ORIANE

Oriane

by
Sigrid de Lima

HARCOURT, BRACE & WORLD, INC.

NEW YORK

ORIANE

1

One day of the year recurs. It is not a day you celebrate or even note as a birthday or a wedding anniversary, and yet it is at least as important as either of these; it elapses innocently and distantly, obscure as a black sun wheeling blindly in the universe of time, invisible and in a sense unreal, the day, of course, which will presently be marked as the day you died.

For you, Oriane Anderton—that is the name of the woman who will concern us here—the last of these concealed anniversaries had occurred precisely one year ago, the day and date had come again. But even on this final day when the minutes and hours of your life swept to the zero, fate cast not the slightest shadow that others might discern. It is known only that as you crossed the treacherous field, you slipped through one of the grassy holes into the cavernous chamber beneath, a drop of some twenty-five or thirty feet to the ruined tiles covered with a rubble of rocks and boulders. The dog faithfully kept watch, barking and barking till one of the workmen came to investigate.

Your friend, Professor Thurby, was waiting with the other tourists near the sight-seeing bus. From time to time he glanced toward the cypress-lined walk that led up to the entrance of Hadrian's Villa expecting momentarily to catch a glimpse of your brilliant yellow-clad figure moving among the trees. Always prompt himself, he fretted at your being late more on principle than out of concern; furthermore, great black clouds had suddenly billowed up in the air presaging a storm although the weather earlier had been fine. The double row of cypresses which he'd always dutifully admired suddenly seemed to him merely so many depressing green markers pointing to the threatening sky.

He removed his glasses and methodically began to clean the lenses. Out of the corner of his unaided eye he could make out the blurry figure of the bus driver moving nonchalantly among the passengers. Eternity sat in that Roman head, he couldn't care less that one or another was always late, even American watches sometimes run slow, there is a misunderstanding or simple irresponsibility. But the other passengers were becoming impatient. Now Thurby had to smile as he heard a fat and reproving voice suggest that they should leave without you: "That would teach her a lesson." As if ever in your life, Oriane, you learned or forgot anything.

Finally they were told of the accident by the goatherd. The same one who had come by in the morning with perhaps a dozen brown and skinny nannies with delicate horns, bleating and tinkling their bells. At that time the group had only just arrived, in fact some of them were still getting out of their bus and the guide, a Mr. Giorgio, had started to say something to the gatekeeper, but that one had hurried away to return with a small tin can. *"Un momento, un momento . . .* Pasquale!"

And there before everyone's delighted eyes and cameras, he had bought his milk, the goatherd milking it directly into the tin. The two men joked, the goat turned her face modestly away, glanced back at the tourists. She had, as you, Oriane, had been quick to point out, the severe, idealistic features of a fanatic. Jumped nimbly forward when she was released, with her teats flapping between her legs.

Now the goatherd came, shuffling and reluctant, led by the gatekeeper to tell them the *signora americana* was dead.

Chance is the motley whose coarse humor we rarely appreciate, directs the fat lady to sit on the too frail chair, puts the banana skin under the lame man's crutch —anyone can multiply the cases; chance determined that the last person to see Oriane alive should be that Professor Edward R. Thurby, English department, Princeton University, a bachelor, middle-aged, fat, bald, timid, sentimental, learned, and helpless. Once he had loved her well—chance works diligently and patiently setting up its practical jokes, conveyed affection into that atrophied breast for the sole purpose, it would seem, that he should see the object of that affection in extinction.

Chance had carefully arranged that these two should be set walking toward each other on the same side of the Via Veneto a couple of days earlier. Naturally they would meet and greet each other. The professor would be happy to discover that his darling was looking well and handsome and almost simultaneously he would remember the gossip about her being in Italy. He would huff and puff and in confusion decide that she had put on some weight since he had last seen her, then go on to remark on it so waggishly that he would be ready to die in the next minute. "Indeed, while I realize that most ladies prefer that their avoirdupois go unnoted, may I take the liberty of complimenting you on your gain."

Up to a certain point we can forgive those who adore us and Oriane had responded with such a sweet and tolerant smile that he carried her off to the Osteria dell'Orso for dinner. There he had proposed the expedition to Hadrian's Villa.

Surprisingly, she accepted at once. "I'm not much on antiquities, you know. But yes, I'd love to go. I really would."

The professor could hardly believe his good fortune. "Then, it's really decided?"

"Yes, of course."

It is one of the few things about that evening which the professor is able to call to mind, since for the most part all he can recollect of their conversation (and it is with real despair) is that it was a monologue. Oriane had allowed him to do all the talking, so like many shy people he had been delighted to talk his head off. About his trip, about the places he'd stayed, about the other passengers on the boat he'd come over on, about factions in the English department, about his students, about his stomach, about his laundry problems while traveling, about the monograph he was preparing on William Morris, about Russia, about Vietnam, about desegregation, about Rome in the age of the Antonines. Thus, out of the three hours that first evening and five hours of the last day in her company, all he can recall is the visual image of the various postures and expressions assumed by a charming, *listening* woman.

Her mobile face with its clear, dark eyes and soft, wide mouth hovered in the shadows of his inward eye as uncommunicative and enigmatic as the stylized portrait on a Roman sarcophagus. By the force of his yearning memory, he might bring back a few of her gestures and mannerisms, recollect her habit of forever putting her hands to her face, nervous, long-fingered, bony hands, hid her mouth when she smoked a cigarette, drooped over her cheek and chin as she sat at the table; he could recall her laugh that was throaty and surprisingly loud. But all these poor, small tokens he'd had by heart in any case through the years.

All of it gone, broken, smashed like so much crockery. He had had to remain for hours at Hadrian's Villa while the workmen recovered her body and then had discovered that no power on earth could induce him to look at her. He'd made the formal identification from the papers in her handbag. And the camera, the Rolleicord in its brown leather case that had miraculously come through unharmed. She must have taken three dozen pictures that last day. From the rings on her fingers and her wristwatch initialed O. A. on the back of its case. And from her yellow clothes.

7

Yellow the color of buttercups and daffodils and sunshine, the last color in the world he would have thought Oriane would choose, not that she didn't carry it off, she had looked splendid, tawny-skinned with glints of reflected gold in that India-ink black hair. "You look like a ray of sunshine, my dear," he had remarked clumsily, but she had died like that, decked out like an oriole. "Look," he remembered her saying as with a yellow-gloved hand she had lifted her skirt a fraction, "I even found a yellow petticoat on the Via Condotti."

In a letter to his sister which Thurby wrote on the following day he opens with a page or two of indifferent news before he speaks of "the very sad affair, the death of our mutual friend Oriane Anderton. There is one point upon which I may be able to prove helpful. That is to say, if there is any remaining ambiguity in the minds of those of you at home as to whether purpose played any part in what occurred.

"I myself think not. Indeed, I would so state categorically. Of course, you, my dear sister, must know that I hold myself ill qualified to look into Woman's heart and mind. As Cervantes has put it, 'What man has assurance enough to pretend to know thoroughly the riddle of a woman's mind, and who could ever hope to fix her mutable nature?'

"I would say, however, that from every outward indication, it appeared that Oriane was of serene and sound mind. She had many delightful and original comments to make of her stay in Italy—she had spent much of it in a town in Tuscany, for which I envy her as these old bones I greatly fear grow too old for the exigencies of a nomadic existence. Of course, again as old Miguel has said, 'It seldom happens that any felicity comes so pure as not to be tempered and allayed by some

8

mixture of sorrow,' and Oriane did quite definitely though of course unobtrusively express her nostalgia and eagerness to return."

At this point, the professor must have laid down his pen for a minute to reread what he had written. For we may be sure that he was fictionizing a bit, that Oriane had hardly mentioned Princeton. Out of discretion, no doubt, since one does not confide one's troubles to a mere acquaintance.

In fact later he would tell us she'd only once shown emotion, and the occasion of it seemed to him so strange that he hadn't known in the least what to make of it. They had been speaking of the town where she had stayed.

Or, rather, heavy with wine and too much food, he had at last stopped his outlandish jabbering on that first evening. While she spoke he had stared at that pale face narrowed by the glossy black hair that fell as straight as rain from a glistening white parting in the center, her brows were too prominent and thick and black, the dark eyes deep-set as two bores in her head, angry and passionate.

She had begun to speak, haltingly and indistinctly, the words muffled behind that hand that came up always to cover that vain, sensuous, pleasure-loving mouth lest it blab that this handsome woman was great-spirited and small-willed.

"I'm sorry, Oriane, I didn't quite catch . . ."

"There was a bandit. He died. They shot him right by the fountain in the town square."

He had looked into her eyes then that seemed to give on a soul from which all the small qualities had fled leaving a crude emptiness of suffering and anguish.

"I had spoken to him only a few minutes before."

9

"He threatened you?" he asked uncomprehendingly.
"Oh no."

The eyes disappeared behind the gleaming white of lowered lids with their shadowy fringe of dark lashes. She appeared to be looking at the salt or at the base of her wine glass. After a moment she lighted a cigarette. "He only asked me which was the road to Rome."

The professor would not dream of mentioning this curious little interchange in his letter to his sister, but no doubt now he resolved to stick more closely to the truth.

"On that last fatal day," he continues on a fresh page, "she was in extremely good spirits. Indeed I might say, we both were. The weather was fine and I had brought along a hamper luncheon prepared by the excellent cook at my *pensione*—as you know I prefer this expedient to taking my chances at the quite possibly expensive and probably inferior *caffè-ristorantes* usually to be met with in the vicinity of outstanding points of interest.

"At another time, of course, I can tell you more about the Villa Adriana, but for the present it is sufficient to say that many new excavations have been in progress since I last visited. For obvious reasons we detached ourselves from the tourist group at the earliest opportunity, merely taking the precaution to set our watches by that of S. Giorgio's to make sure we might have a ride back to Rome. Indeed we had already been unfortunate enough to have had to listen on the way out to that gentleman's glib travesty of a lecture on the Second Century Empire. Quite possibly I may have bored Oriane with my own lecture on the same subject, but if so, charming woman that she was, she never gave the least indication!

"At noon we were grateful to find a fine olive grove near a small farm which looked extremely picturesque from the spot we chose to picnic. (As I pointed out to Oriane at the time, I have no doubt that the picturesque qualities might have proved less attractive on closer inspection.) However, as I say, from our vantage point the modest earth-colored buildings, set about with brilliant flowers, were charming. It was from this farm the lad came out to warn us of the treacherous hill beyond the grove, it contained, he said, numerous caves and cisterns from ancient times. He was accompanied by a lively half-grown shepherd dog that subsequently remained with us. (Presently you will discover why I mention this here.) We thanked him for his trouble and I gave him a few pennies, much to his delight (the Italians always amaze me by being so openly surprised to receive what they patently expect), and this one returned a little later to present us with a bottle of really excellent wine which was made at the farm. All of this, as you can imagine, put us in a very pleasant frame of mind. The young dog was happy to stay with us since the contents of the hamper were more than adequate to our needs and Oriane was pleased to give him some scraps. It was the dog, however, I'm afraid, that proved to be Oriane's undoing.

"As I have noted, it accompanied us when we resumed our rambles and after a while Oriane began to be concerned as to whether it would know how to return to its home. I assured her that the creature must know the region better than the best guide, but she continued to fret. At last, she insisted that she wouldn't be happy till she returned the dog herself and, as she knew how anxious I was to see the Valley of Canopus, she made me agree not to go with her. For this, of course, I shall never forgive myself.

"The last I saw of her, she was striding up the path, the camera dangling by its long strap from her shoulder while she carried in her free hand a short stick which from time to time she lightheartedly threw for the dog to retrieve, or held up at arm's length for him to jump at."

NOTA BENE:

One does not use thread to stitch shadows—so we may plead that what was is not and thus the infinite variants of could and might no longer must give place to intransitive and intransigent being; the dream exists in dreamlessness equally with the reality that is dreamed away. We grant you that, Oriane, for all the good it may do you. All your fictions we transcribe here as the soberest truth and let the created stand equal to the actual. Nor need you thank us for our liberality, Oriane. When all is said and done, you will only have gained the freedom accorded the mouse by the teasing cat.

2

The fact is our passionate and headstrong and foolish heroine is forty-nine years old—this particular statistic the good Professor Thurby naturally overlooked. Not being exactly a spring chicken himself.

So it follows that Oriane's vanity case is sadly over-packed with endocrine creams and royal jellies, night masks and chin firmers, make-up bases and powders that cover, color tints and hair conditioners, et cetera, et cetera, down the list of Helena Rubinstein's bag of tricks to gild the withered lily. Oh, this is not to say that Oriane isn't handsome still—handsome is as handsome does, and she does handsomely.

In a sense, that is, to have acquired an eager lover and elope with him to a hill town in Tuscany, this is handsomeness personified. And the eye can only be further ravished as it discerns the lineaments of Gratified Desire superimposed upon the sweet Italian landscape. So what of the cynics in the wings who alternate their snickerings with sighs of pity.

Well, this well-seasoned inamorata would have for her opposite number one Mark Norwood, aged twenty-six, who is chiefly known hereabouts for his good looks and for the fact that he was newly married to the lovely Miss Theresa Anderton, Oriane's only child—a more delicately embarrassing impediment to true love is hard to imagine. Since there is no accounting for taste, we may refrain from comment that this young man should prefer his wine from old bottles. As we would see, panic and mortification both play their parts when he manages to break away from his former entanglement at the last possible moment. All of which the mother of the injured daughter would be able to conveniently overlook. To necessarily overlook.

Necessity, yes—one always answers with a slavish yes to necessity—Oriane was not mean-spirited or lacking in courage, that goes without saying, her faults were of another order, but here she needs must assent, just as a congress of beeves in a shambles must ratify the decree of the butcher.

So these two, ill matched, ill fated, would be immured in their happiness, so to speak, whatever it is they'd actually feel they'd be too deeply committed to call it by any other name: only local and temporary irritants would contravene. Oriane suffers on and off from a stomach complaint; the first *pensione* in Florence is too primitive, the next is too expensive, a third too crowded. The weather is rainy, or too cold, or too hot, or too changeable, Oriane catches a bad cold. They would also find that there are too many diversions in Florence that distract Mark from his work. Finally they would hear of Friani, a little ancient town out in the hills where no one ever goes (or so they might erroneously suppose) ; after visiting it and luckily (or unluckily) finding rooms in a small hotel they would decide to settle there.

Which is by no means so modest as it sounds, since the hotel is one of the towering *palazzi* for which the town is famous. But the actual need not keep us long as we snoop and spy after "our pair of lovers," following them boldly into the rooms they occupy. Enormous rooms, complete with balcony and damp-stained frescoes on the ceilings. Swallows—or at least they both assume they are swallows—black, noisy birds, roost behind the shutters. Oriane, nervously awake at dawn, watches them flying at the windows like enormous moths. It has become an obsession with her never to let Mark see her before she has applied her make-up, so that the slightest stirring that he makes in his sleep arouses her and sends her off to her mirror and pots of paint. Then she returns to sit next to him against the hour when he shall finally awaken.

The birds swoop and soar, a swarm of banging omens, for from time to time they strike the iron shutters with their strong wings; she sees them indistinctly as patches of blackness against the narrow streaks of colored light that penetrate the blinds.

Then she will turn her head and tenderly contemplate her beloved sleeping, that dear face now curiously helpless as slumber seals up those bold, imperious eyes which by their size and brilliance dominate his waking face. There is something of a pout in the way his pale lips are softly closed. She dotes on them and on the way the light falls on the smooth, hard curve of his cheek, then she views the sweet hollow of his neck adorned with a little pale mound of Adam's apple. His arms are flung over his head, smoothly muscled in repose, big hands, fingers lazily curled over the rosy palms.

But not for long, perhaps there is some instinct, some sense that never sleeps that makes him withdraw from that hot, caressing gaze, after a few minutes he has turned on his side, his back to her, presenting her the bristling brush of black hair snuggled among the bed-clothes.

Such a small rejection, what implacable vanity is there in her that is wounded by such a mote; tears come to those beautiful mascaraed eyes and her face stiffens and empties of all expression. Oh, Oriane, if your friends could see you now! Or Giles and Tessa. Blink-ing, still, dumb as a brute under the full impact of sudden anguish, she waits for it to pass, knowing with the cold clarity of the doomed that it would never pass, that in time no anodyne would be sufficient, but for the present she could find a curious comfort—she could look at her watch and tell herself that in America it's five hours earlier, they sleep, everyone she knows is asleep, that distant, invisible, hostile audience which is the only one she knows about or cares about is still asleep, for there it is three in the morning.

Putting cream on her hands for the second or third time that morning she discovered a little scratch just below the knuckle of the right thumb, a tiny mark

17

perhaps three-eighths of an inch long covered with a little, narrow scab; the hurt had been so slight that she had no idea when or how it had happened, and it was also healing itself without her even noting it.

If she hadn't been looking at her hands she would never have known about it at all. If she could only stop worrying perhaps everything would get better like that. She forced herself to smile and looked absently at her suitcase on the floor near the window.

From where she was sitting at the dressing table, she could see the end of it, massive and brown, by no means new, rather shabby in fact; it sported a peeling sticker from the President Taft Hotel—she had never in her life stayed at a President Taft Hotel—well, perhaps Giles had used it on one of his trips. And exactly when was Taft president? It was the kind of useless question she liked to pop on her friends, and none of them except dear Professor Thurby would be able to answer it. Oh Jarry Holt, perhaps, she's old enough to have remembered his administration. Elizabeth Blaine, no, the Weirs and all the rest probably no. They were all there that day when she gave the garden party to celebrate the Chinese dogwood's coming to bloom. Oriane clenched her hands together, rubbing the little scab on her knuckle. A little homesickness is only natural, she told herself, one need only think of something else.

Ah, the President Taft Hotel.

The bottom part of the sticker was torn off; probably the name of the city had been written there. It was impossible to tell where the President Taft was, the picture of it looked like the picture of any hotel. A big square building with lots of windows. Just above the tear it said: RATES REASONABLE. BATH IN EVERY . . . then the tear.

Oh!

She would never see any of them again.

It was at the party she gave for the Chinese dogwood that she met Mark again. She had invited all those people because for a long time before that they had done almost no entertaining. And it was a beautiful day, the weather was just perfect, everyone said so. The Blaines, the Weirs, the Misses Crory, the Trotters, Ed Thurby, who had brought along a young graduate student, a Negro who was reputed to be brilliant, but Libby Blaine, who always made a beeline for anyone distinguished, had grabbed him right away. Oh yes, Mrs. Norwood had come, don't forget her. But Mark hadn't come with his mother, he arrived later.

They had all been outside on the back lawn and Oriane had gone into the house to lay out the tea cakes when he came to the front door. She remembered him standing outside the screen, very tall, but the light fell on him in such a way that he appeared to be merely a dim shadow-man pricked out in the cross-stitching of the wire screen: the notion pleased Oriane and she was laughing when she greeted him. Ten weeks later he was engaged to Tessa.

Sometimes Oriane leaves her sleeping Mark alone and goes down to the desk to get the newspaper and see if there is any mail. Once she came upon a little boy standing in the hall quite by himself outside the water closet. He looked too young to be by himself, not more than three, but even at that age there was something definably American about him. She stopped, surprised, then she heard a woman's voice from within call out, "Charlie, are you still there?"

"Yes."

The door opened a crack, closed. Then a minute later the woman called out, "You haven't gone away, have you, Charlie?"

"No."

"Charlie!"

"What?"

"Nothing, dear, I just want to know if you're still there."

The little boy looked up at Oriane. He had a bland, rather stupid little face, thin with very light hair, almost white. He was sucking his thumb.

"Hello, Charlie," said Oriane finally. "How are you?"

Of course the child had no answer. The woman inside called, "I'll be right out, Missus."

"That's all right."

"I won't be long. I'm sorry to keep you waiting."

"Really . . . I don't mind." Of course she had no reason to wait. One of the few private bathrooms in the place was connected to their room, but she suddenly wanted to stay here and listen to that flat American voice, New York by the sound of it, in this remote place.

"Would you keep an eye on Charlie, please, Missus?"

"Oh surely."

"I worry about that boy. He runs away . . . he's still there, isn't he?"

"Yes. Don't worry, I'm watching him."

"Cat got your tongue, Charlie?" Oriane asked uncertainly. The child stared at her so that she was filled with uneasiness, but when she spoke to him he turned away, ducking his head in a cringing motion under his hunched shoulder.

"All the time he's running away," said the woman

within. She was rustling the paper now. "It's a stage they go through."

"I know."

"I don't know at what age they're worst," continued the mother. She opened the door and came out. She was a big woman with a tremendous amount of thick, brown hair cut in an unbecoming square bob with flat bangs over her forehead. Now she squinted down at her small son as if to make sure that he hadn't disappeared. "All I know is that this one's the worst of the lot. Believe me."

"Yes."

"Up you go." She bent down and picked up the child, who looked even smaller and paler in his mother's arms. He also looked different and strange and apart to have sprung from such a woman, he was too frail and delicate.

"I have one too," Oriane said suddenly.

"What?" The woman looked at her blankly.

"I have a baby of my own." She gestured toward the end of the hall. "Back there in my room. He's asleep."

The weird and wild stratagem to keep these two a moment longer proved quite useless. The woman merely nodded her head, "When they're asleep, then they're good. Well, bye now. And, say, thanks for keeping an eye on Charlie." She strode down the hall.

Well, it didn't really matter.

She would have become bored with the woman very quickly if she had had to talk to her. What she really disliked was talking to the clerk at the desk. He was a short, dark man with small hands and feet and a soft, fat body. He was practically bald but what hair remained was black and heavily greased. His eyes were tiny and shifty and he had a peculiar intimate way of speaking which set Oriane's teeth on edge. Of course, Oriane reflected, he knew from their passports that she and Mark were not married and with every word he uttered he seemed to be proclaiming his discretion and broad-mindedness.

"Ah, Madame is up early today. For the newspapers. Immediately I will look to see if they have come." However he didn't move a muscle except to show his teeth in a smile that was not a smile.

She waited passively with her eyes lowered. There seemed to be a perfect silence around her—there couldn't have been, people were passing in and out of the lobby, the elevator descended, opened its door with clashing jangling, a telephone on the desk began to ring and a maid in a dirty apron came over to answer it, all of these rendered soundless by her preoccupying embarrassment. She watched as in a dream the clerk's small hands finally disappear into a drawer behind the counter and come up not with a sheaf of newspapers but a postcard.

"It's for Madame. Yes?"

She stared at it stupidly. A postcard that was addressed in green ink to Mrs. Mark Norwood. Suddenly she heard all the sounds around her, roaring, oppressive random noise.

"Yes?"

A joke. But who could play such a cruel, despicable, completely unfunny joke. A picture of Scolly Square, signed Betty B., no enlightenment there. "Hi, now you know the significance of rice how about joining us in the Vineyard. We go the 21st, loads of love, Betty B." Postmarked Lynn, Mass. Forwarded by the post office in Princeton.

(Hours later it would come to her: Lynn, Mass., she had written that on one of the wedding invitations.

Betty Bones. The girl whose name had launched a thousand jokes, Tessa had said.)

"Oh yes," she said finally, and taking the card by the smallest corner dropped it into her handbag. She could tell that the clerk had read it. What difference did it make? Then as she was turning away, he called her back. "Madame wanted the newspapers?" He managed to make it sound like an accusation. Her first notion was of a conjuring trick, for there next to his elbow was the little pile of newspapers. Never mind. She reached out to take one just as he reached to give her one and their hands touched.

"Scusi."

Now she was hurrying back to the stairs, better to take the stairs than to wait for the elevator—it was only two flights up; stairs heavily carpeted, wild, garish design, Moorish in inspiration, probably made in Holland or Germany or some such unlikely place, so heavy and thick that it turned the steps into a series of ascending soft mounds. His hands had been hot and dry, in the trifling contact she had noticed that and it filled her with distress.

Up past the turn in the staircase, the lobby was left behind and hidden, and the carpeting ceased abruptly in the middle of the flight, so now her heels clicked noisily on the bare stone steps. When she reached the second story the elevator had just arrived, its gates were closed, however, and the operator had brought it to a stop about a foot below the floor level. Oriane stopped, out of breath, to watch him start it again only to stop it about two feet too high. She gestured to him not to bother, but was greeted with a flood of Italian explanations and someone began shouting from below.

"I prefer to walk," she said flatly in English and again started for the stairs.

"*Signora!*"

He made another try and missed again. All the same he opened the gate saying "*Prego,*" imploringly. It should have been funny but she wanted to cry. Why did it have to be so complicated merely to get a morning newspaper!

She came back down the stairs but she simply could not bring herself to step down that twenty or so inches into the swaying elevator cage.

"*Un momento, signora.*"

He closed the gate again, ascended grandly past her to the upper stories. Now she would walk. As she got to her floor the elevator got there too and stopped only about six inches too high.

He opened the gate with a flourish, but turning her back on him and squaring her shoulders she stalked down the hall feeling as though she were walking away from a loaded revolver. Just before she reached the very end and her own room, she heard the gate crash closed; it was only then that she noticed the slight difference in the hallway, the doors were painted a different tone of yellow and the room numbers were all in the two hundreds—the third floor was three flights up.

Nothing for it but to retrace her steps and climb the stairs as quietly as possible and count herself lucky that the elevator operator was now having trouble stopping at the first floor. She reached her room at last and was at once inside leaning against the door, painfully trying to get her breath and whispering over and over again, "My God, Mark, how I love you."

3

Poor Oriane attracts malice as a sunflower attracts birds. Twittering and fluttery we flock to put in our two cents' worth whenever her name comes up. Peck peck peck peck as if this provided our only nourishment, voracious as lean, bold jays. "Dear Oriane," someone would say and we'd be off like a gaggle of geese and incidentally I cannot think of a single instance when the speaker failed to insert a "dear" before Oriane's name.

Sometimes dear Oriane would have written one of us a letter. It would be full of descriptions of olive groves and vineyards, crumbling castles, white oxen and the rest of it, the whole informed with the implied heady aura of passion satisfied and dreams come true, as is to be expected, and we would respond like so many good little red hens, planting our corn, so to speak, and eating our muffins as though that were the soul of virtue.

Nor did the news of her fatal accident discourage our chatter—on the contrary, we battened like condors on the poor scraps that remained. It's all very well to say that charity begins at home; it wasn't beginning with us, certainly not until every other possibility had been exhausted. We each, of course, had our own theory as to "what really happened," erecting vast, teetery structures out of the fragments of truth we could catch sight of over and around and through our own preconceptions and complacencies. Then too, while none of us would have considered herself vengeful, we demanded that symmetry that retribution gives. Or to put it another way, in our heart of hearts we sought to discover some gesture in which we could read if not an expression of regret, at least, as one of us put it, "a simple recognition of the suffering that her actions had brought to those closest to her."

And this in spite of the fact that we found that so blatantly grieving husband faintly ridiculous. There he is, a middle-sized man, paunchy, with thick white hair and a beard like General Grant's; he wears steel-rimmed glasses, the kind that have recently come in style with young girls who wear them with their granny dresses. They make him look old-fashioned, which, together with an upright carriage and the rather dusty, shabby black suits he wears, gives him the air of an old school-master and by extension all the kindly, sweet, high-minded qualities of a Mr. Chips. Quite a setup for poor (dear) Oriane to deal with by running away from.

Of course, in the beginning, we were moved to pity by this snuffling, wheezing apparition that settled down damply in our living rooms. He was fond of calling on each of Oriane's friends to complain tearfully of his loneliness, but at the same time regale us with the most embarrassing details of his twenty-five years of marriage. Then he would explain heavily that more than anything else, it was his pride that had been injured, claiming in one breath that he would welcome her back with open arms and that he would never forgive her as long as he lived.

Now Oriane's daughter, who we easily assumed had been deeply scarred, offended (though that is probably too strong a word for it) in an opposite manner, refused all sympathy by the simple expedient of not being around to receive it, and, according to one of us who had seen her, she put such a bland face on the whole sorry business that we ended by concluding that she was either a pudding or, according to the psychological clairvoyants among us, a mass of emotional abnormalities and repressions.

I mention these things merely to show our temper, because the little anecdotes about Oriane that will follow here, while doubtless true as far as they go, are colored by our present bias. Likewise, we find it hard to admit that we were as blind as moles never to have grasped what was so patently right under our noses. Or if not blindness, it was our presumptions and assumptions that misled us, thus we permitted ourselves to be grossly fooled by the externals, for in these Oriane was not only one of us but she was the one that any of us would have cited as that abstraction, the most typical of us, we saw ourselves in her, our virtues, our faults, our compromises.

Furthermore, we made the mistake of taking the most unstable, the most evanescent and transient of beings, a woman, and equating her with a table that may show nicks and scars and signs of wear but remains substantially unchanged.

Rather Oriane was, as we all are, not one person but a series of persons, and we should practice the common witchcraft of discovering her in each of her incarnations, no small task, since we too are passing imperceptively through stages of being, the small miracle that everyone performs without thought.

Arbitrarily now I will speak of the Oriane I first laid eyes on when I came to Princeton in 1956. It was late August or early September, a few weeks before the term at the university began. Steve had received his appointment in the previous spring but he had been teaching in the Indiana University summer session so we had put off house hunting in Princeton until this late date.

Neither of us was familiar with Princeton and we had done a prodigious amount of walking around. Finally I had got tired and I sat down on the stone parapet near the physics building and Steve, who had an appointment with someone in the art department, left me there to wait for him.

From where I sat I could look across the tennis courts, where there was one lone player in view, at the Colosseum-like Palmer Stadium half hidden by a double row of slender elms. The whole place had that astonished, unawakened quality of abandonment. All under a serene blue sky; here were the winding paths, the shaded nooks that cried out for students to sit on the grass, the shining lake yearning for canoeists. Everywhere I looked there was no sign of life save for that lone player on the court below. Actually her being there at all implied that at least one other person was abroad, but her opponent was invisible behind the wall on the far side of the sloping road.

But she played with style and flair and enormous skill, holding the racket in her left hand, against a white dancing ball that seemed to bounce out from nowhere. She was a lean, dark-haired girl, trim in a handsome white outfit and dazzling, never-worn-before sneakers. She leaped, she reached, she paused to serve, graceful but with that particular strong, hard grace of an athlete, not dancer, sent the ball speeding into nowhere. (I could not even see the net from where I sat.) And the sight held me spellbound—I suppose it was the illusory inexplicableness of this white-clad figure bounding and fanning the air, anticipating, retreating, lunging forward, a brass-band concert of motion.

Finally the game came to an end. My player disappeared for a few minutes from my view and then I saw her walking below me on the path, her racket in a press under her arm. She ran lightly up the steps and stood beside me on the upper walk. Now I looked curiously into a face that had no trace of that freedom and careless power that I had seen on the court. A face that was furrowed and furious, I thought of an American Indian deprived of his realm, this face presented itself frowning, its black brows drawn together, the mouth set in a hard, defiant line.

I stared and our eyes met for an instant. I found myself stammering quite unnecessarily that I had been watching and that I had enjoyed her playing. I found myself denying it when she said she was not in very good form. "I'm quite out of practice—that was nothing really."

Then she was saying, "I played in the Eastern Women's Finals at Forest Hills in 1946."

"Oh yes?"

"I was in the women's singles."

"Oh, that's wonderful. Congratulations." I felt foolish but there was something so peculiar about the way she looked and talked, I wanted to hear what else she would say. "Who was your opponent?"

She looked at me sharply for a moment. It was so quickly done that I couldn't be sure, but I thought I saw a wave of anguish pass over that hard, dark face. "Pauline Betz," she brought out slowly.

"Yes."

But at that moment Steve appeared on the path that led into the campus. "Hello there."

I turned thinking he was talking to me, but it was this stranger whom he greeted.

"Do you know each other?" I asked in astonishment.

"Yes, this is Mrs. Anderton. I was telling you about Giles Anderton, I met him the last time I was down. We all had coffee together."

Her manner changed at once. She was very much the polite faculty wife talking to the newcomers. Of course we hadn't had a chance to find out how we liked it here. Yes, Princeton is very pretty. When we got settled we must be sure and come over. Was there anything she could do to help us—the cool offer that implies that it must be rejected. There were some really interesting people around. Of course it's a small town after New

York, but you really never stifled to death because you could always get away to the City on weekends.

The usual smooth chatter, meaningless polite oil. She did offer us a lift in her car which we were happy to accept because we had been given the address of a sublet in a place called Stanworth, would that be far out of her way? Not at all, indeed she had several friends there and she was sure we would like it. Of the short ride there's nothing I particularly remember. She drove down a road back of the campus and told us the names of the various buildings as we passed them. I thought her voice sounded bored and wooden, still, that is neither here nor there.

Suddenly about two blocks from Stanworth, on Bayard Lane, she stopped the car at the curb. "I'll let you off here."

"Why sure, thank you ever so much."

"It's only a little way more."

"It's quite all right. We're so grateful."

We got out and turned around to wave at her. The street was wide here and empty, the big trees on either side laced their topmost branches together in a green cathedral ceiling. I had one more look at Oriane's face, withdrawn, anguished now that she thought herself alone, her mouth set in a defiant downward curve. Her lips moved soundlessly or perhaps the sound was drowned by the roar of the engine. The car plunged forward—she drove with the same ruthless force I had seen on the tennis court—bucking a little as she shifted gears and blowing up a miniature whirlwind of fallen leaves and dust in the gutter. I saw her raise her hand, waving as the car sped away, leaving a dim, blue plume of exhaust, up the long avenue only to brake sharply and turn in two blocks ahead on what I later discovered to be South Stanworth Drive.

✳

I regret that this is such an unkind and obscure little story about Oriane, and to this day I cannot really explain it. At that time (mistakenly, I now think) I put down her behavior to snobbishness, the more particularly in that the next few times I met her, her conversation was littered with the names of the famous people who lived in the vicinity, exploiting the smallest contact with them, such as passing So-and-So, the Nobel Prize winner, in the street, or seeing another celebrity eating an ice-cream cone or sitting two seats behind a third "great" at a concert. Once she discovered I was a writer, she did not rest till she took me to see John O'Hara's unmarked mailbox. Or she pointed out the house where Einstein had lived and remarked with easy familiarity that it was "just what one would expect inside." Slips for the plants in her garden came from the big outlying estates whose owners, she told me, were "lovely people really."

I suppose it's a measure of Oriane's personality that one didn't hold all this against her. Indeed, I remember being rather pleased when, some time later, Oriane rather imperiously invited us over for dinner. Of course she didn't refrain from adding a needling "We're having some friends in, they're not important people but I think you'll find them amusing." Leaving me with a vision of how she catalogued her acquaintances and just where we fitted in. However, once I knew her better, I realized she was merely trying to sound sophisticated and worldly. It went with her cooking with herbs and

32

shopping for sale-priced French wines, the empty bottles of which she saved, soaking the labels off the better to appreciate their subtle coloration and suave contours.

The Anderton house is some six or seven miles out of Princeton, a sweet New Jersey colonial that is more than a hundred years old. It's been renovated at various times so that the different rooms are of different proportions and styles, but on three sides the trees grow so close to the house that its broken lines are camouflaged with greenery. On the fourth side the windows give on a spectacular sweep of lawn, for the house is set on the top of a small hill and from here there is a pretty view of the gently undulating countryside.

That first evening struck me as rather strange, though I would later discover that it followed pretty much the same pattern as others I would spend with the Andertons. The "amusing friends" were ill assorted and had little to say to one another with the result that terrible gaping silences kept falling on the company and finally, in desperation, I think, Oriane had us all listening to her quite standard collection of folk-song records. I recall that at one point Giles Anderton produced a Spanish guitar that had belonged to his grandmother. It was a beautiful instrument but he could play only two or three chords and he sang "Sweet Betsy from Pike" with long pauses between the verses while he asked Oriane for the words that had slipped his memory.

This was the first time, I remember, that I had met Giles. To my surprise he was a rather short man—Oriane was so tall that I had assumed that her husband would be a six-footer at least—and he appeared to be a good deal older than she. He came to the door carrying a Martini that clashed decidedly with his Mr. Chips manner, as did the too red cheeks and the overly bright eyes behind their steel-rimmed spectacles. The beard was there, large as life, and also the full head of white hair brushed up from his forehead in a wavy pompadour. He greeted us with languid good humor saying, "I'm the man of the house, come in, come in. I don't know this little lady yet but I'm sure she's been invited. I'm pleased to make your acquaintance. Do come in.

"Oh Professor Greene. Of course I remember you now, Stephen Greene, the artist. No relation to Hetty Green, I don't guess. Or Graham Greene. Greene's a pretty popular name I guess. Let me tell you first off I'm very bad on names. Oriane mentioned that you were coming, of course, but I thought you were somebody else, and I'm very bad on faces too."

Then he tried awkwardly and one-handedly to help me off with my coat, surrendered me fussily to Steve and suddenly handed me the cocktail.

"Why thank you."

"I know how it is to come in the door of this house," he remarked.

We were standing in the hall, which was long and low, paneled in dark wood, a massive Victorian staircase flanked one of the rear walls; at the far end was a glass door against which glimmered the dying day. One didn't expect such a hall from the simple exterior of the house, and the feeling it gave one was vaguely depressing. Oriane had done the best she could to brighten the place up by placing a number of large copper vases along the two side walls. These contained a veritable forest of cut branches, oak, maple, beech and dogwood with their lacquered autumn leaves, here and there were the brilliant berries of fire thorn and bayberry or

34

the white note of birch. It was through all this foliage that Oriane appeared now like a lamia in a skin-tight black satin gown that left her virtually naked from the waist up.

Actually, of course, some layers of thin, ivory-toned crepe covered the tips of her breasts, but this too was so scant that the shadowed, tender crease between them was clearly visible. She wore a long strand of glassy pearls around her neck, one end of which disappeared into the top of the dress, and as if this weren't enough she had placed a soft-headed purplish chrysanthemum between her breasts. From time to time during the evening she would remove the flower and fondle it with her fingers, then hold it out for one or another of us to smell. "When I was a girl," she'd say, "my mother always put the crushed, dried leaves of chrysanthemums among my underthings. It was a trick she had learned from her mother."

Now she stood before us with the combination of a child's pride in a new dress and the embarrassment of nudity. Then she laid her hands with widespread fingers over her milky bosom. "Oh, there you are," she said.

"And all taken care of," said Giles.

"For heaven's sake, let them come in first."

"When you come in, you can have another," he said to me. The four of us stood there a little strained waiting in a weird way for me to finish the cocktail. I guiltily raised it to my lips. Over the glass I could see Oriane and I felt about four years old drinking up all my nice milk under my mother's reproving eye.

Then Giles was taking the glass from me. "You see," he said lightly, "Oriane doesn't approve of me, but there's this to be said, she *understands* me."

"You are absolutely right, Mister," Oriane returned. Then she took my arm and ducking a little to avoid the branches remarked to me, "I feel silly in all this skin and I've more pins in this damn dress than a porcupine."

*

As I have said, this was not a particularly successful dinner party. Giles was a heavy-handed bartender and his over-generous drinks made us sleepy rather than talkative. Then too, Oriane's cooking was so exotic that most of us went hungry (later on I got used to her peculiar dishes but they took getting used to). The women got themselves into a conversational group that allowed itself to be dominated with a discussion of domestic problems though I did break away from that long enough to talk to a fat little instructor in the English department, Dr. Thurby, about his recent tour of England. I did notice then without thinking about it particularly that Dr. Thurby never took his eyes off his hostess the entire evening, but I don't think he spoke to her more than to greet her when he came in. He would, I suppose, have said good-bye as well, but this brings me to the main thing that stands out in my mind about the evening.

Now I know very few people who, when they are not having a very good time, simply get up and leave. The tendency is quite the contrary. If a situation is strained and awkward we hang around that much longer as if the simple fact of our presence could hide our boredom. Thus Oriane's party went on and on. We were hearing for the third time the troubles a Mrs. Denny was having getting her washing machine repaired and the men weren't doing much better with Giles around to finish off any conversation with a crashing near-quotation such as "These days sure try a man's patience," or "Some things fool you every time."

All of this was so soporific that none of us noticed for some time that Oriane was no longer there. Then we thought of all kinds of normal explanations and some of us went to look for her in the kitchen ostensibly to "help her." We only found Tessa there with a little friend busily raiding the refrigerator but she informed us, "Oh no, Mummy isn't upstairs."

Presently in a kind of panic we began to leave. Still there was no Oriane to say good-bye to. We stood around with our coats on as if that would bring her back and all the while Giles kept up an appearance of not noticing his wife's absence, in spite of the fact that several of us asked him to convey messages to her. "Yes, yes," he'd say and look so blank that one had the impression that he hadn't understood a word.

This went on for twenty minutes or half an hour before we finally managed to get out of there. Steve remarked as we drove off that he thought the reason we had been invited was that Mrs. Anderton wished to enroll in his drawing class at the university. That, of course, was impossible, he had told her and now he added with some asperity that he didn't think I'd see much more of "my," as he put it, Oriane. As it turned out, however, within fifteen minutes we found ourselves sitting opposite her in a highway pizzeria.

It was a typical highway diner with a counter along one side and small booths on the other. Chromium, formica and leatherette were much in evidence as well as an enormous jukebox; the windows were dim with steam and the air was blue with cooking smoke; it catered obviously to the unfastidious tastes of college students and all-night travelers, but the evening had been such that the moment we saw its lights, Steve and I agreed to stop there.

We were just finishing when looking out of the steamy window I caught sight of a white convertible that slammed to a stop in the parking area in front of the diner and from it emerged immediately that tall, thin Indian figure, closing the door behind herself with such force that the whole car rocked. Oh, I would know her anywhere, that narrow head held so stiffly on its long neck, those strong, thin, limber legs and sure feet that hurried so swiftly over the rutted gravel.

Oriane had taken off her fine clothes, bare legs were thrust into some old sneakers, a too small gabardine raincoat fell short of her knees, and in the sleeves gave up at mid-forearm. She raised her chin defiantly as the stale air and bright fluorescent lights within struck her. Her brilliant eyes stared at us as at strangers. Nevertheless, after a moment she came over to our table. "Huh" —a gruff sound like that—"I'll join you if you don't mind . . . I should say 'we' . . ." in a mumbling undertone.

We turned and looked at the boy now, whom neither of us had noticed before though he had followed Oriane into the diner. He was tall, rather gangling, fourteen or fifteen years old, wearing a much-laundered sweat shirt and jeans, his pale, good-looking face was dominated by shining dark eyes and a great bush of curly black hair that tumbled over his forehead.

"But I forgot, you don't know my friend here," Oriane continued. "I think that I have made hundreds of introductions in my time but none of them were important. They did not take, as the doctors say when they inoculate you with smallpox. I love my friends and I bring my friends face to face and say you must be friends too. But my friends are turtles and they will not come out of their shells, they are snails, they are clams, they might as well be little stones they are so hard and still. But I do not really know the secret of making friends. Sooner or later they find me out and I find them out, little stones that I call my friends, so this is not really a friend that I will introduce. He is a person I know. That is all I will say. Come here, Mark, I want to introduce you to the Greenes. Greenes, this is Marcus Antonius Norwood."

The boy shook hands with us solemnly, and I, for one, found his grip hard enough to make my bones crack. "Only part of that's my name," he muttered almost inaudibly.

"Oh Marcus, I can't resist you. Look at all that hair!" Oriane put her hand lightly on his head and he shook it off like a young horse. This made her laugh.

"We had a lovely time, Oriane," I said to change the subject.

"Yes, yes," she returned impatiently. Then sat down. For a moment she seemed to be studying her long, narrow hands, which she placed side by side on the table. "Order me some coffee and a Danish," she said to no one in particular, which resulted in some confusion as both Steve and the boy tried to accommodate her. Ignoring them, she carefully raised one hand and placed it on top of the other, then wriggled the two extended thumbs. "I suppose your husband told you that I wanted to enroll in his class."

"Yes, he did."

39

"I think his answer would have been different if my name were Mrs. John O'Hara."

"That's not true, Oriane. It's just that the class is limited to the students at the university."

She looked up at me, scowling, then after a moment her face cleared and she smiled. "You know, I'm awfully glad you said that. I really am." Then abruptly she turned her face away and began to weep.

It was the boy who took over then. He fetched her coffee and bun from the counter and teasing and coaxing began to get her to take some. He was marvelous: solicitous, gentle, firm, tender. He had all kinds of things to say to her that cheered her up. When we left she was smiling uncertainly. But as we got in our car and looked back, the two were sitting opposite each other laughing their heads off.

4

The village of Friani is close enough to Florence for Oriane to take the bus in two or three times a week. She went for every reason and none. She went to shop, she went to sight-see, she went in order to give Mark time alone with his work, she went to lose herself in a larger place, she went to sit in the Piazza della Signoria at one of the little tables and drink bitter Campari and listen to the chattering around her that was in French or German or Swedish or Hindu and every other language under the sun. She went also, I think, in order to have something to write home about.

She liked the bus ride as much as anything else, in an

ancient, rickety vehicle with a marvelous, raucous horn that played three notes in a quaternary bray and a stuck accelerator that had lost its spring so that unless it was specifically made inoperative by the application of the clutch, say, or a turned-off ignition the bus was always ready to go at top speed, which if not impressive on ascents was thrillingly so downhill. Hosts of angels, gods and saints must have preserved those passengers who hurtled through the air in that flimsy rocket, this conglutinate congeries of fatigued-metal parts and baling wire, of broken glass and worn rubber, this wretched insult to the mechanical genius of our time, in this scatheless wreck that managed to defy every law of physics and probability, not once but four times a day and six days a week.

So, as we have said, every three or four days Oriane laid out a few lire for a trip to heaven's gate and back. Combed, brushed, powdered, rouged, perfumed, dressed to the nines, she was a bizarre sight in the crowd of black-clad peasants who made up the usual passenger list.

Now, Oriane had taken this trip a few times when there appeared the Man in the White Coat. With the cameras. It was an extraordinary white coat, if not as white as it once had been. It was made of heavy canvas which had undergone a rubberizing process that left it stiff and absolutely impermeable. There were certain vents and flaps and flies and holes to keep the wearer from melting away of his own body heat which made the garment even more outlandish-looking. Adorning all this were a multitude of long leather straps that crossed and crisscrossed the young man's chest and back, all of them attached to small leather cases that contained

42

cameras and equipment. He was carrying a small canvas bag that quite possibly contained more of the same and as he walked down the aisle with some notion of making himself small, he held it above his head. This had the astonishing effect of raising his coat, which not being able to give over his chest because of all the straps expressed itself by extending its tails like two tremendous wings. Oriane, who carried a purse that was the size of a pillowcase, hid her smiles in its capacious darkness, but the Italians, who certainly found the sight as funny as she did, managed to maintain a solemn mien, their faces simply drained of all expression and for once they became as quiet as so many good children in school.

Now the unfortunate young man taxed their politeness to the limit, since he proceeded down the entire length of the bus, his arms over his head and the two "wings" extended, but once there, not finding a seat that satisfied him, he turned around, swishing his extensions into various hats and faces as he did so, and solemnly returned to the front of the bus.

"*Permesssssssso?*" he was hissing at Oriane suddenly. I don't know why she was so surprised—such a man would most naturally choose her as a seat mate, for she was certainly as strange in this company as he, and a moment later, when he had finally stowed his bag away on the overhead shelf, lowered his arms, folded his wings so to speak and sat down beside her, the rest of the passengers nodded their heads and resumed their conversations as if they had merely witnessed the inevitable finish to an entirely conventional rite.

These two, however much of a kind, took some time to start talking to each other though they both knew they must end by doing so. Oriane was determined not to give the young man any help whatsoever though she scrutinized him thoroughly if surreptitiously. He had an odd smell which disconcerted her somewhat, not unpleasant, of wet dried grass, of all things, though rather mustier. All the straps and thongs squeaked a little with his breathing, nor was it easy for him to sit still. His long legs were cramped in the narrow space between the seats, moreover he displayed an unmistakable yellow streak on the shrieking descents from the hilltops, his feet slammed themselves on the floor as if on imaginary brakes and his freckled hands became white and rigid grasping the back of the seat in front of him.

Now the bus inched up a long incline, it wheezed and puffed and threatened to boil over, but otherwise proceeded at such a modest rate of speed that the young man relaxed with more squeakings and shiftings, little suspecting that by far the most hazardous down journey was imminent over the crest of the hill. The bus was rather warm and he proceeded to undo some of the loops and buttons that secured his coat so tightly under his chin.

In so doing, he trespassed a certain amount with his elbows and shoulders into Oriane's section of the seat, but all the sibilant *scusi*s that followed didn't serve to start a conversation, nor when careening down the other side of the hill did all his heartfelt exclamations and imprecations in English, though they confirmed Oriane's impression that he was an American.

Now about an hour out of Friani there was a little roadside café where the bus almost invariably stopped for an unscheduled half hour or so. The driver left the bus and disappeared inside and the passengers likewise descended, some of them merely to stretch their legs, but quite a few partook of what refreshments were available. The café proper was a dark little hole with a greasy counter, but it also boasted an adjoining court-yard with a couple of rickety tables and chairs set out on the hard dirt under some dusty plane trees.

On this day Oriane took a chair at one of the tables and the young man, after fussily not being able to decide whether or not to bring his satchel along and finally deciding to do so, followed her and *permesso*ed himself into one of the vacant chairs at her table. Previ-ously she had only examined his face from the side, to be impressed by his great, arching, sensitive camel-like, llama-like nose. From the front this same nose appeared to be larger at the top than at the base, which gave him a curiously ovine look.

"Baa," said Oriane to herself, "I've picked up even worse in my long life than this," so after she'd ordered herself some totally dreadful *caffè espresso,* she re-marked kindly to the young man that his coat was very unusual.

He blushed immediately with pleasure and informed her that it was called a hunter's mac and had been purchased in a shop in Southampton. He had worn it steadily in rainy England, not-so-rainy France, waterless Spain, arid North Africa and now in sunny Italy because it was awkward to carry. However, it had all these wonderful pockets in it for knives and guns and ammu-nition and such which quite easily held much of his photography equipment.

No, Chester Dundee, for that was the young man's name, was not a professional photographer. It was, he said with a delicacy that seemed oddly inappropriate, a "hobby." "I mean what one might call a hobby though I don't like to use the word myself. What I mean is I work for A.T.&T. Have for seventeen years. I'm thirty-five though everybody thinks I'm younger. I've been called 'boy' lots of times by men who are younger than I am. But a few years ago I got this camera bug. I mean I found I like taking pictures. I've got pictures from all over. Nothing fancy like these contest winners. I mean pretty soon I'm going to take a picture of the bus on sixteen millimeter though I don't guess you know what that means. It's this camera here." He tapped a leather case over his fifth rib.

He was a most guileless and confiding creature and before they returned to the bus Oriane learned that he had spent most of his childhood in an orphanage, that his teeth were one hundred per cent perfect, that he never wanted to marry or settle down, that everything he owned would fit in a suitcase, that whenever he had been a year or so in one place he'd apply for a transfer and go somewhere else, that his dearest hope was before he died to visit every country in the world and live in every state in the Union. This trip he had done eight countries, on previous trips he'd done all the countries in North and Central America and seven countries in northern Europe.

Thus they chatted along pleasantly enough. When the bill came he assiduously calculated his share including half of the tip. Oriane was amused but there was, after all, she reflected, no reason for his treating her. In the bus, he continued his own history, which on the whole was a relief to Oriane, for she had not the slightest wish to discuss her own with him. Of course he did interrupt himself on some of the downhill courses, but such is the adaptability of man that, although he still clutched the back of the seat in front of him and placed his feet heavily on the floor, he now faced his dangers in tight-lipped silence.

It was after one of these that he asked the question of Oriane that she least cared to answer.

"D'ya mind telling me how old you are, Miss—er—a—Missus?"

"Missus," she answered coldly, "Mrs. Anderton. My husband has work to do and he doesn't care to tag along after me when I go shopping."

He waved his hand vaguely. "Of course, of course. Shopping's always bad and over here you have to do all this bargaining thing." Still he was looking at her sharply waiting for the answer to his question.

"I don't mind bargaining."

Now he seemed to have changed the subject, but not at all. "Well, I had a friend. He died. We used to play this game, I guess you'd call it, I mean before he died, we used to play it. That is, we used to guess how old people are. You'd be surprised, we got pretty good at it. I mean practically every time we'd guess pretty darn close to the truth; that is, when we could get a person to tell you how old he was, it would turn out to be just about what we guessed.

"Well, I've been doing that a long time now. I mean I never stopped. I'll bet I've guessed about a million times in the past ten years, and I'll say that I was right in the vast majority of cases. Well, what I'm trying to say is that I don't mean anything personal asking you how old you are." He paused delicately. "I mean, of course, if you don't want to tell me it's all right, but I'd appreciate it if you did. I mean I've already guessed how old you are so I want to see if I'm right or not. Like in science."

"Twenty-one plus," Oriane answered evenly.

"Forty-nine. Am I right?"

"No."

"You know, the funny thing, there are more ladies who will tell you than men, though it's supposed to be the other way round. You can tell though, and you can tell if they're telling the truth. For instance, you're pulling my leg, so to speak, when you say you're not forty-nine."

"No." She disliked this man now more than she had ever disliked anyone in her life but there was no escape from him.

"Do you know how I tell?"

"No." In spite of herself: "How?" Hair, hands, crow's-feet, neck, shoes. Which proclaims the passage of years, rings on a tree, teeth in a horse's mouth, lead in the rock, sand on the ocean floor.

"Not the hair." But she wasn't to know. "You see those two ladies over there?"

"Yes."

"One's thirty-four and the other's twenty-seven."

"Did you ask them?"

"No, but I'm pretty sure I'm right, though it's hard to tell on foreigners. But I've been looking at them all of the time I've been talking to you. Would you say I was right?"

"I have no idea."

"You're a deep one."

"Sure."

"Well it's all right. Some people are what I call sensitive."

"Yes," said Oriane firmly and the subject was once and forever closed. The Duomo in Florence was already in sight and in five minutes they would be there and she need never see him again. Now he had the look of a puppy who knows he has misbehaved but hasn't the foggiest idea of the reason why. Finally he reached out and put his hand tentatively on Oriane's arm. "Please, Missus, wouldja do me a personal favor?"

What now? She would see him personally in hell first.

"Wouldja take my picture when we get out? Standing in front of the bus? I would appreciate it if ya would."

"I'm not much at taking pictures."

"There's nothing to it. All you have to do is point the camera the way I'll show you and push the shutter."

"Aren't you afraid I might drop it or something?"

"Oh no, Missus, you wouldn't drop it." He put so much reproach in his voice that Oriane wanted to burst out laughing, and that nose of his, like a camel's or a llama's—not really, like an enormous white rabbit's, pink at the tip, constantly in motion—and the one eye she could see, round and distressed, she could imagine herself holding up a bunch of carrot tops to that huge, sad, ultrasensitive nose. Oh the poor God-damn orphan, well she'd take his picture if he wanted.

"Okay, I'll take your picture" (call me anything-for-peace-Oriane Anderton) "and I won't drop your camera, I promise, but I'm not much at taking pictures so you better set it and everything."

The bus was going down a tree-lined street in the outskirts of Florence and she could not have felt better. She always felt good coming into Florence. The Friani bus had an informal terminal at a gas station. One walked from there across a little square that was decorated by a large, hideously modern fountain and took the local bus into the old part of town.

"I guess you have quite a few photographs," she

49

added kindly. It was the nearest thing she could think of as a bunch of carrot tops, because even after she had relented that white-rabbit profile still looked alarmed.

"Oh yes, I do have a lot. I think I must have a million, or close to it. I keep them in boxes."

There wasn't time to say more because the bus had finally jolted to its stop. It roared and shuddered as the driver threw out the clutch, then finally subsided like a dying reptile when the ignition key was turned off. All the passengers except Oriane and her young man were standing in the aisle long before this happened and they jostled out shouting long farewells at the driver as they passed.

Now Oriane hadn't known what she had got herself in for when she had agreed to take the young man's picture. Once they were off the bus, he walked around it several times, looking for the best vantage point. Then there was the problem of open shade. A not-very-healthy tree spread its spindly branches over part of the bus. It created a kind of shade, but not very much, since the bright Italian sunshine had no trouble at all penetrating these all-but-ravaged leaves. Out came the light meter and the young man took a vast number of readings from it during the next five or ten minutes while Oriane watched the local buses take off for downtown and reflected what a goodhearted soul she really was.

He was ready at last and standing her in such and such a place handed her his camera all set up, then telling her to wait ran awkwardly back to the door of the bus and striking a manly pose commanded her to "Shoot," which she dutifully did.

He ran back to her looking happier than he'd looked all morning and fussily took his camera back looking wistfully into its mysterious black-shuttered lens before finally snapping the metal guard into place.

"I'll tell you a sort of a sad story."

"Really I must go now."

"It's about a fellow I asked to take my picture like you did just now. He was a nice-enough fellow from Hartford, Connecticut, I remember that, and I remember he told me he was a college man. Well, I set up this wonderful picture down there in Naples, me standing in front of the cathedral. Well, this fellow said he'd take it, but he didn't after all though I didn't find out till later when I had the films developed. You know what he did? He just pretended to take the picture of me there smiling and looking good. I said 'Shoot' just like I did to you, and he said 'Roger,' just like he had, but then when I wasn't looking he swung the camera around and what he took a picture of was a dirty old man peeing against a wall."

"I'm sorry. Oh I am sorry."

"He just did it to be funny, I suppose, but it wasn't nice."

"No, it wasn't nice, it was awful. Just awful."

"Sorta pathetic."

"It's awful, it's awful."

Another bus had stopped by the hideous fountain and she ran on awkward high heels not to miss it. "Goodbye," she said over her shoulder, but she wasn't running to catch the bus, she was running so she wouldn't cry over the poor simp who had stood there posing with a big smile while the stranger from Hartford played a dirty trick on him. But why do I care? she asked herself. Why do I care? Why do I always care? But she cared terribly.

51

Then as she rode mournfully downtown she fell to wondering if Mark had ever been to Hartford, Connecticut. Probably he has, she concluded, almost everybody has, if only to pass through.

5

Those eyes of his, blue and empty as the sky, strange eyes in a way, so lacking in mystery, the pupils were unusually small in that pale azure field, a handicap, for his night vision was poor; the blank eyes imparted a blankness to his face. The eyes, they said, he had from his mother, that poor little unknown who had died when he was born.

In Hartford, Connecticut.

It took Oriane almost a week to make the connection, though she was enough of an amateur psychologist not to be surprised that she had "repressed" this particular fact about Giles for so long. However, the name Hart-

53

ford, Connecticut, was there, stuck in her brain grinding out the syllables like a cockeyed phonograph: Hartford, Connecticut, then a dry laugh, Hartford, Connecticut, laugh, Ha ha ha ha Hartford, Connecticut. . . . His laugh, one of his jokes. Giles, God knows, is packed with jokes like a grandmother's trunk, personal, family, insider jokes so that strangers listening to his guffaws think he's a loony.

The joke, such as it was, in this case might be explained; his mother had meant to go to New Haven on that memorable day but she had inadvertently asked for a ticket to Hartford. Her absent-mindedness undoubtedly derived from the fact that she was going into labor and the poor lady probably never did discover her mistake: an ambulance rushed her from the station to the hospital, where she died giving Giles to the world two months prematurely. This part of the "joke" gave Oriane the horrors, but Giles always shrugged and said brashly he could not possibly love a mother whom he had never known.

Giles had been brought up by his paternal grandmother, a very strong-minded woman from Newburgh, New York, known inappropriately as Mopsy. It was Mopsy, no doubt, who had originally discovered the humorous side of puerperal fever. In any case she had loathed her daughter-in-law and like any self-respecting witch was complacent about her victim's sad end. Sometimes it seemed she had taken her grandson out of spite, but she guarded him jealously even from his father—her only son. The latter eventually remarried and settled in California. Thereupon Mopsy reversed herself and had nothing but praise for that heroic progenitor of this unworthy little boy.

Giles, boy and man, learned very well that all his faults had been inherited from his mother along with his eyes, and his faults were fairly numerous. He was lazy, he was greedy, he was stubborn, he was timid, withdrawn, untruthful, resigned to the fact that whenever he did as he was told he would do it wrong; he grew to be a youth who was only passably good-looking, a good head of hair that would probably last him all his life and those strange eyes were his best points. His mouth and chin were both small in proportion to the rest of his face, which his grandmother considered girlish and she could hardly wait for him to grow old enough to cover them up with a decorous General Grant sort of beard. Of course, Mopsy had worked hard on him and she'd taught him to be cleanly, serious, thorough, mannerly and thoughtful of the "little things," fetching shawls and glasses of water or holding doors open for ladies. In due time she chose engineering as a profession for him though she would have preferred medicine or the law, but in all honesty, as she called it, she didn't think him prepossessing enough for either; she chose the school, Rensselaer Polytechnic Institute (not too far away) in Troy, sent him a monthly check that was small enough to guarantee that he would not have a very good time.

Now Oriane enters the scene—she's only ten or eleven years old, but no matter, we have to believe this part of the story because Oriane herself set such store by it—she arrives in patent-leather shoes and pigtails, a copybook under her arm and jacks in her pocket and falls madly in love with the thin, pale boy who's home from college and is brought by his grandmother to call on *her* grandmother one fine July day—afterward there was a fireworks display over the Hudson and Oriane stood beside her beloved struck silent by the grand spectacle, precociously imagining herself a victim in a bombardment being saved by this hero (who at a later time only recalls, yes he did watch some fireworks from somebody's front lawn and there was a little girl there, shy— he had asked her how she liked school and how old she was, which only made her blush to the whites of her eyes).

This is all nonsense, of course, easily explained nonsense as Oriane's two older sisters were nineteen and twenty and considered belles, so the baby of the family had no trouble imagining herself at least "in love." But though toys are usually put away as the child grows older, this one didn't happen to be. Thus, among the photographs that she would carry around in her wallet to the last day of her life, there is one of herself taken at thirteen or thereabouts, a lean, bright-eyed girl probably not greatly changed from the inamorata of two or three years earlier. She has, you might say, an old-young face, thin, intense, as you would expect, with a sharp chin, eager, and at the same time there's a quizzical look to the tight-lipped smile and an answering irony in the very black eyes that look out from under the long bangs of a newly acquired (Oriane would explain) Dutch-boy haircut. All of which does not go well with the dark serge middy and pleated skirt, long black stockings, ankle-high laced black shoes and the rather awkward pose at the top of a short flight of steps.

It's impossible to say what there is about this picture that pleased Oriane so much that she would carry it around with her in her purse almost forty years later, though one might suspect that it greatly appealed to her when it was taken since it probably represents only partially what she really looked like and rather more particularly what she aspired to look like at the time. And who wouldn't value a quizzical smile and an ironical expression in the eyes, being thirteen or so years old and already deeply in love for two or three years!

✳

The robe was beautiful. White with a tiny over-all design of gray, pure silk—*seta pura*—material handsome enough to make the most distinguished neckties in the world, the Italians extravagantly made it up into a man's robe. Fit for a king. Now it hung casually on a hook on the inside of the bathroom door.

Oriane had bought it for Mark in a little shop in Florence, happily and recklessly paying a fortune for it. Told herself, for pure voluptuousness nothing compares with silk and it's really a present for both of us. And she did get her money's worth, every time she laid eyes on it, she experienced a little thrilling chill of pleasure.

This morning she had discovered a tiny rip in the stitching at the cuff, so she had laid the garment down on the unmade bed and gone to fetch her sewing basket from the bureau. The bathroom door was open and she could hear the water roaring in the old-fashioned pipes. She hummed as she worked, happier than she had been for a long time, so pleased was she with Mark's robe and even for the small office that she was performing for him. Six stitches and a knot and it was finished. She put aside the needle and thread and stretched out the robe as if to display it, arms out, belt loosely tied, skirt evenly aligned. Then suddenly she laughed and embraced it.

There was a knock on the door and Oriane eagerly

ran to answer it, but it was only the maid bringing breakfast on a tray.

"I am going mad," she said bitterly.

"Prego, signora?"

"Oh nothing, nothing, put it there on the table." Oriane gestured impatiently, and though the maid spoke no English she understood well enough. By this time Oriane had caught sight of the big suitcase against the wall, the one with the sticker from the President Taft Hotel. Yes. Rates reasonable. Bath in every . . . then the tear. Could it have been the hotel in Buffalo? Was *that* hotel the President Taft?

But good God, why Buffalo? It could have been in Ha Ha Hartford, Connecticut. She bit her lip and followed the maid over to the table by the window and looked down at the dome-covered plates as the maid set them down.

"Due cappuccini, due uove al latte, frutte e pane," she ticked off the dishes carefully.

"That's all right, everthing's there."

"Va bene?"

"Sì, grazie molto," Oriane managed distractedly. She looked at the beautiful robe on the bed in a vain attempt to divert her thoughts. The maid withdrew. *Grazie,* Oriane repeated to herself. *Grazie.* Gracious, Buffalo! It may very well have been in Buffalo. She remembers everything else about that hotel except the name . . . bath in every . . . then the tear. She had shut herself in the bathroom and cried.

While Giles had walked back and forth, back and forth saying, "It's nerves. Nerves, pure and simple," in the exasperated overwrought tone of a newlywed.

But what a room for honeymooners! It was long and

narrow and dingy. Its one window overlooked the dreary kitchen courtyard. The bed, Oriane would swear to the end of her days, was made of tin, some metal, painted to simulate wood, it clanked and banged and squeaked like an old car on a washboard road, there was a matching chest of drawers and a large golden-oak chair that screamed at you everything you might need to know about Grand Rapids. Oh yes, the Hotel Taft, or whatever its name was, had fine and splendid rooms, but this was the room that Giles had written ahead for and reserved. Stingy. The hot tears stung her eyes and coursed down her cheeks, she stuffed her handkerchief into her mouth so as not to cry aloud. He had always been stingy, he always would be. Of course, he had always preferred to eat scrambled eggs at her house when he courted her, or take her for walks in preference to any outing that might cost money, but such stinginess on a honeymoon! Ah yes, Mrs. Giles Anderton, you have a lot to wake up to. Even to the fact that stinginess is not the worst fault in the world.

She washed her face and combed her hair and put on a little powder. In those dim, unappreciated days a little cold water and a dusting of tinted talc was all that young face needed before it showed itself to the world; she was able to go out and smile at him simperingly, take his arm and descend courageously to the enormous dining room.

Designed apparently for political conventions or trade fairs, the room, virtually empty now with twenty-five people in it—half of them waiters—appeared large enough to house a cathedral. There were acres of white tables all supplied with silver and glassware and cone-folded napkins. Four or five waiters helped them get seated, handed them outsized menus, lit the candle lamps, pulled out a chair for Oriane's wraps—all she had was a light scarf so she put her evening bag on it as well, rushed up to fill their glasses with water. "We won't eat here often," His Stinginess spoke. No one in his right mind would eat there often.

The maître d'hôtel knew a honeymoon couple when he saw one and determined to make the most of it. A handsome, florid, stout fellow with the scruples of a pirate, the slyness of a fox and the ho ho ho type of heartiness of a department-store Santa Claus. He cowed and flattered them by rattling off the menu in French, he reassured them by telling them what the dishes were without appearing to, he was decorously impressed by the bride's beauty and culture—she had managed "vichyssoise" casually and correctly—he praised to the skies Giles's choice of wine which he "misunderstood" was the most expensive available (Giles, of course, had ordered a split of the cheapest on the menu with a large aside to Oriane that tonight he thought they ought to have wine with their meal), and poor Giles was too intimidated to correct him.

Now our jolly friend having cast his victim into a blurry state of complete despondency over the wine order proceeded to draw up for them a bill of fare suitable to a king's purse and a Gargantua's appetite. "A meal you will never forget," he said happily with glistening, doting eyes. (Indeed, they never would.) Every dish that he mentioned he rolled around on imagination's tongue. "Sweet little oysters flown in from chilly Maine . . ." Giles was staring at the salt and Oriane recalled that he couldn't abide the slimy things. "Tender Swedish herring in cream perhaps?"

"The small tomato juice" (20¢ extra), said Giles firmly.

"*Potage du jour*—vegetable soup. Ah, I can tell, Madame wishes the vichyssoise" (50¢ extra), "*very* good. Prime roast beef *au jus,* buttered new green peas and mashed potatoes"—it was an aria that Ezio Pinza would not have been ashamed of. "Or *poulet*—southern-fried chicken . . ." The resources of the kitchen were strictly average, which had nothing to do with the fine frenzy going on in the dining room.

Giles was perspiring freely, in an effort to keep track of the figures on the right-hand column, no doubt. An older and wiser Oriane would have noticed the flushed face and the little vein that was standing out on his forehead like a lightning mark, but alas her eyes were on the menu and now she said dreamily, "You know, I think I would like some oysters."

"I never knew you liked oysters" (Maine oysters 75¢ extra).

"I adore them."

"Then Madame would like the large order" ($1.25).

"No, no," Giles exclaimed in desperation, "you won't be able to eat so much."

"Well . . ." she hesitated, there was something in his voice—she should perhaps defer to her new-wedded lord. She looked at him over the top of the menu for one second.

"The small order, please," she said meekly.

"Not just to please me, Oriane."

"No, I think you're right, the large order would be too much."

Now, perhaps all would have been well. Giles's face relaxed, he might even have smiled at such a dutiful wife but in that instant the demon waiter engaged in another one of his pyrotechnics—quite literally. With a large, impressive wave of his arm, the gesture of a Toscanini calling into play an entire orchestra, he suddenly reached forward with a little flame cupped in his hand. Giles had absently taken out a cigarette and he was merely being offered a light, but startled and taken unawares he jerked his head back, knocking it painfully against the back of his chair. Poor Oriane not realizing that he had hurt himself continued smiling dreamily for some moments, and though afterward she was full of concern and sympathy, he would have none of it, puffed at the thanklessly lighted cigarette, producing the great clouds of smoke of an angry dragon.

It goes without saying that the meal was a complete failure for both of them. Sauced with his fury, all flavors were as one and the wine though passably good was a heavy one and Giles drank too much of it, grimly determined to have his money's worth and it made him as logy as a winter fly. They ate in silence except when Giles made such unpleasant remarks as "Oysters make me think of somebody's spit on the sidewalk." But he downed everything that was set before him with a sullen determination that forced Oriane to do likewise.

With the coffee, the maître d'hôtel returned jolly as dear old Saint Nick. On his tray along with the coffee service were two little glasses of cognac which they hadn't ordered.

"Compliments of the house," remarked that indefatigable one. "I trust you enjoyed your dinner. Monsieur and Madame are newly married I think," he went on to say.

"Yes," Oriane answered softly, and glanced at her watch. "It's exactly twenty-eight hours."

"Lovely, lovely." His head cocked on one side, his lips pouted and his eyes rolled merrily. "Then you will have spent last night on the train."

This made Oriane blush prettily, and he set the brandy before her with a flourish. At this point, Giles suddenly got to his feet, he looked so pale that it seemed as if he were about to faint or be ill, but he turned on his heel and walked steadily and determinedly from the room. Surprised, but carefully refraining from showing it, the maître d'hôtel quickly finished with the coffee service, flicked away two or three crumbs with his napkin, refilled the water glasses and discreetly withdrew.

In the beginning, Oriane rather enjoyed sitting there in lonely state. She toyed with the brandy, which cast a bright little golden shadow on the white cloth, which trembled when she touched the outside of the glass and set the liquid within in motion. The food and wine had revived her amazingly, she could even contemplate their dreary little room with equanimity. Giles had been right, it was "nerves" that had set her off so. After all they would only be there to sleep.

Sleep—the maiden bride can only bear to contemplate the word for a moment, then she hastily pours out the coffee and stirs it with an agitated spoon. Then she notices that an extra coffee spoon has been placed on the table and, with elaborate carelessness and cunning glances around the room to see if she is observed, she drops her handkerchief over it, then after a moment, slips both into her purse.

A remarkably poor little theft but so neatly done that she can't help but be pleased with herself. Now she gazes at the room as if to commit the whole scene to memory. Its very emptiness and vastness please her. The nearest diners are tables away from her, and at this late hour there are only the dawdlers left, so even the waiters are a long way from her view, clustered around the serving table at the back carrying on subdued conversations among themselves.

Her friendly enemy, the maître d'hôtel, has himself sat down at the back eating an enormous meal.

By leaning forward and craning her neck, Oriane discovers that she can see into one of the pair of plate-glass mirrors attached to opposite walls, and all at once the whole scene is multiplied into a tricky infinity.

Oriane smiled, both at the effect and because she had realized without pride and without false modesty that she was looking exceedingly pretty. But what had happened to Giles? Still, she hadn't been keeping track of the time, and probably he hadn't been gone very long. Now she glanced complacently at her watch, it was a tiny new one that her mother had given her as a wedding present.

And she waited. And waited. Twenty minutes, half an hour, still he didn't come. Quite soon she drank up all the coffee in the pot, they would order more when Giles returned; she smoked several cigarettes, although in those days one cigarette was enough for a whole evening, she read the menu over and over, she opened her purse and found a circular about Niagara Falls which, for want of anything else to do, she practically committed to memory. The waiters continued to talk among themselves though periodically one or another detached himself from the others to bring more and more food to the maître d'hôtel, the golden second hand on her watch continued to make its sweeping circle, the candle at the centerpiece guttered and went out. What on earth could have happened to Giles?

Perhaps he was ill. Perhaps he had gone to make a telephone call, perhaps he had gone back to the room, and she was supposed to meet him there. Perhaps, perhaps anything. She curled her foot around the leg of the table. At any rate she could wait in this place forever and no one would ever notice it.

Time here was the drugged, glutted, palpable element of waiting rooms, overhead light of high noon or midnight; she stared until she had half mesmerized herself at the flaring spill of coffee in the saucer; the very air that she breathed was sour and flat from lack of circulating; she realized wide-eyed that she was very tired, Giles seemed to have vanished from the face of the earth.

Could he really have been so angry about the oysters? About the wine? Had he run out of money? But he had lots of money, she had seen his billfold stuffed with money. He had put it down on the dresser when he had changed his clothes and she remembered thinking it looked like a sandwich with a green filling, also she remembered distinctly seeing him replace it in his jacket pocket, where it made a slight bulge. In despair she reviewed all the small events of their grim dinner. He had been angry about the oysters and the wine, now she was quite sure of it, but would that have made him run out, and just when the maître d'hôtel had brought the cognac, he had distinctly said it was free, and Giles should have been pleased about that!

Flushing with the creeping beginnings of anger, she had the money for the tip and the rest of the bill could go on their hotel charges, after all they were staying there, there was not the slightest reason for her to wait any longer; her breath became labored and her eyes grew hot as she thought of the ignominy of getting up and leaving. She was looking at her watch to put a deadline on her waiting when the door opened. But it was not he!

It was a tall, thin man dressed entirely in white, no doubt it was a uniform of some kind, but at the moment it seemed peculiar, like the distinctive costume of a play-acting ghost to set him off from the drab-coated living.

His voice was sepulchral too, though he leaned jauntily against the table talking with a waiter who had hurried up to inform him that the kitchen was closed. "All I want, buster, is some light coffee and a roll if you have it."

Oriane drew in her breath sharply, in two minutes she would leave; she put her handbag upright in her lap and surreptitiously began hunting through the bottom of it with her fingers for a pencil. The man in white stared at her surveyingly and she looked boldly back armed with her fury against Giles. Spook!

Mercifully now her mind becomes blank, she doesn't remember and was hardly aware at the time how she reached across the table and downed in one fiery swallow the brandy at Giles's place, then she took the bill that was discreetly face down on a plate beside it and hurriedly scribbled Giles's name on it and their room number. Then she took all the money from her purse and placed it on top of the bill. Groping blindly she took her wrap from the chair, put it around her shoulders, before she quietly got up and left the room. She must have stopped at the desk and asked for a key, then have taken the elevator to their floor. She has no recollection of that at all, nor even how she entered their room, undressed and got into bed. She seems to have slept because she remembered waking up in the morning.

Giles was there sleeping on a chair. When he finally roused himself he turned on her such a look of bland innocence that she thought she must have dreamed everything. Then, sweet and friendly-faced and without apology he methodically undressed and lay down beside her. He was very gentle and thoughtful and patient with her and at last she thought she found repose in his arms.

6

Spook Hollow wasn't named for the spooks that lived in the house. Nor, as Giles never tired of saying, was it in Eerie County. It got its name from the little creek which was actually no more than a long artificial conduit from a spring at the head of the basin formed by the sloping lawns to a round, black pond some fifty yards lower down. However, it had been constructed so many years before that it had taken on the aspect of a true stream, shallow and meandering, its clear waters gliding noiselessly over the round pebbles at its bottom; the fact that it had no apparent source—the spring merely welled up from a hillock of grass—and that the pond, which was quite deep, drained invisibly into the spongy soil of the meadow below the hollow gave the water a magical, mysterious quality.

According to legend—imparted to Giles by the workmen who were renovating the heating system shortly after they moved into the house—the pond was bottomless and an Indian princess had drowned herself in it when her true love died in battle; there was a wild rose growing on the spot where she was supposed to have stood before she threw herself in. Actually the pond was perhaps fifteen feet deep and Indians had vanished from the region at least a hundred years before it came into being.

There was one great tree beside the brook, an enormous witch's besom of a willow, and a tangled patch of Osage orange, sassafras and witch hazel, and, at the upper end, a little grove of birches. Giles and Oriane were delighted with this spot and Giles, who was given to this kind of elocution, heavily informed his wife that she must never change any of it, that he would seek it out for the rest of his days, coming here when he was sad, when he was weary, when he was elated and merry, or when he had merely had too much for dinner, to commune with the quiet, spooky brook.

Nor did it ever cease to astonish him that he owned it, that it was possible for anyone to own a brook, water that welled up from the earth and disappeared into an apparently bottomless pond, owning not to the middle of the water, but to its edges, a technicality which theoretically enabled him to prevent thirsty cattle or sheep from drinking, or boys from fishing or swimming, rights he never dreamed of exercising, but rights nevertheless, which, in an access of feeling when he caught sight of the little boy who lived in the next house, he ceremoniously bestowed on the astonished child—the privilege of swimming and fishing in the water whenever he liked. Mark, for that's who the boy was, thanked him very politely and then fled. Except for frogs and tadpoles there was nothing in the pond to fish for and he had long since been forbidden by his mother to go near the place, because she considered it dangerous.

Oriane laughed when Giles told her of the episode, for she could visualize only too well her big, pale husband looming up under the willow tree saying, "My dear boy, please make free with the water of this pond. We would only be too happy to permit you to bathe in our pond, or if angling is your fancy, please do not hesitate to make busy with your rod and reel." She was only mistaken in that she imagined the little boy as being snub-nosed and freckled, a Mickey Rooney type of average American youngster. Nor did she find out for some time, till the incident was well forgotten, for she was too busy settling in her new home and too shy besides to call on the residents of the little house on the other side of the Hollow, and they—the Norwoods, Oriane eventually discovered that was their name from the postmistress—kept very much to themselves.

One mild autumn afternoon when Oriane was walking down by the pond she stumbled over the root of a tree; in trying to recover her balance, she only made matters worse and she fell heavily on her side, twisting her ankle as she went down. The wind was knocked out of her, she dazedly tried to stand up, but was prevented from doing so by the excruciating pain in her ankle.

She stripped off her shoe and stocking and soaked her foot in the cold water of the pond, but it was some time before she realized the gravity of her situation—there was no one at home at the time to miss her or look for her, and the only other house nearby, the Norwoods', though closer than her own, was still almost a quarter of a mile away.

Actually, she told herself, she wasn't so badly off: fortunately she was warmly dressed, and when Giles did come home, it would eventually occur even to him to look for his wife, or since four-year-old Tessa was visiting a little friend, that little friend's mother might spread the alarm when Oriane failed to come and pick up her daughter.

All she would have to do was wait and it would make an adventure to talk about afterward. "There I was absolutely helpless, down there in that Godforsaken place and all I could do was wait." Her spirits began to revive and she began to picture herself in really darker straits as she imagined herself looking back in memory. Of course there were mosquitoes and probably snakes— water moccasins quite possibly. She moved back from the water and sat on a fallen log. She did see a chipmunk, which after all is a cheerful little creature, but it put her in mind of water rats, then it occurred to her that as night fell there would undoubtedly be bats flying around.

Of course she would suffer from hunger, she thought complacently, though she need not go thirsty if she could bring herself to drink the polluted-looking water from the pond. But also she was in some pain. The injured ankle quite soon began to swell up, and she had bruised her side as well. The log she was sitting on was damp and increasingly uncomfortable, so presently on her hands and knees she crept to a higher spot and lay down on some soft-looking but rather prickly long grass. There, in spite of everything, she fell asleep.

To be awakened by "my infant Saint George, by my very young Lochinvar coming out of the West," she would say afterward with a mixture of irony and earnestness. It was Mark Norwood, then aged around seven and one of the handsomest little boys Oriane had ever laid eyes on. Of course, over the years she greatly romanticized the incident, and while we may assume that a good-looking man was probably a good-looking child, the impossibly lovely face that Oriane recalls that she saw on awakening probably belonged to some Pre-Raphaelite painting, with a halo of dark curls setting off those princely features.

As for the boy, he had the large imagination of a lonely child, and he was happy to think of himself as a hero, especially when later the fruits of his heroism included free and unlimited access to Oriane's cooky jar and stores of soft drinks, not to mention the gifts of books and toys that she came to lavish upon him as time went on. In other words this would be the beginning of a lasting if anomalous friendship between these two, it was also the beginning, though Oriane would not realize it for a long time, of the great love of her life.

At the time, however, their meeting almost never did take place. When he saw the lady awaken, Mark shyly withdrew, and it took her a great deal of calling and coaxing to get him to come close enough for her to explain to him that she had hurt herself, and please would he go and get help for her.

"I'll help you myself," he said (adorably, she thought) , "I have very strong arms."

She looked at him doubtfully, however. "There's no

one at my house. But perhaps your father or your mother . . . I'm quite big you see, and I can hardly walk."

"Father's at the store and Mother doesn't come here."

"Maybe she would if you tell her I need her."

"No, she wouldn't." He spoke with such finality that Oriane couldn't persist. Instead she got to her feet, resting all her weight on the sound foot, but she was terribly stiff from lying on the ground. She smiled thinly. "Well, it'll have to be you then." He looked terribly small and frail to her. "We'll go to your house, it's nearer."

It seemed like a long, long way at that, but with frequent stops they made it all right, Oriane was probably less badly hurt than she had supposed or perhaps little Mark was stronger than he looked. They didn't talk very much as they went along, saving all their breath for their exertions, but Oriane found that she was rather enjoying the boy's company. He was full of "I'm sorry"s and "Oh, excuse me"s which gave him an old-fashioned, carefully brought-up air.

They approached the house by the back yard, which was weedy and neglected. Discarded metal objects and toys rusted in the long grass. A cockeyed clothesline rack occupied the space near the back door, and a few yards from this was a big, black circle of cinders where rubbish was burned from time to time. There was a beaten-dirt path that led to the front of the house, and it was down this path that Mark guided Oriane, ignoring the closer, but to him inappropriate, entry through the kitchen door. The front yard was at least picked up and it boasted two rather rangy hydrangea bushes set primly on each side of a straight gravel path that took one from

73

a gated opening in a tall privet hedge to the steps of a very wide veranda that ran along the entire front of the quite small brown-shingled house and down the full length of one side. Mark took Oriane up these steps and deposited her on a wicker chair on the porch and then went on into the house to notify his mother that she was there.

Oriane waited rather a long while with some impatience and some amusement too, for within the house she could hear great runnings around, openings and closings of doors and a certain amount of muffled shouting back and forth. Obviously, Mrs. Norwood was not prepared to receive unexpected guests, and although Oriane in her present predicament didn't fall into this category, Mrs. Norwood felt otherwise.

When she finally appeared, flushed under some hurriedly applied powder, in an elaborate dark-blue dress, her hair freshly groomed, one could see how eager she was to make a good impression. Mark came out only a few moments after his mother, equally transformed, wearing a clean white shirt and black trousers, his curly black hair wetted down and combed, his face washed—an office he performed for himself, as one could observe from the shadow of grime that stopped at and marked his jaw line.

Mrs. Norwood was a plump but worn-looking woman. She had fine dark eyes with long curling eyelashes, and eyebrows so thick and dense that they had originally met over the top of her nose. This condition had been inexpertly remedied by electrolysis which had left the area with enlarged and reddened pores. Her mouth was prim and tense and naturally so tightly closed that the lips were almost hidden entirely, her nose was sharp and angular with two very deep grooves extending from it to the corners of her mouth.

Now she was all smiles and fawning good nature. In a tiny, breathy voice she told Oriane to please step into her humble abode, that she was terribly, terribly sorry about Oriane's accident, that Oriane must have some tea, that she must forgive her for the condition of the house, that naturally she wasn't expected, but she was terribly welcome all the same and what a frightening and terrible experience she must have had to be hurt like that and all alone down there in the Wilds. (She didn't exactly lisp, but the "terribles" that were so obsessively present in her speech were pronounced "ter-wible.")

She herself worried terribly when her little boy went for walks in the woods, but wasn't it simply providential that he had gone there today? Yes, Oriane must feel free to use her telephone and of course when Clayton got home he would be only too happy to drive her home in their car. (Clayton was James Clayton Norwood, who was called Jim as he preferred by everyone except his wife.) But Oriane must come in; Mark dear, you must help Mrs. Anderton. And she must have some tea. Tea is so terribly comforting. She had a very special orange pekoe, her mamma had always favored orange pekoe.

Under the circumstances, Oriane, who would much rather have stayed where she was, had no choice but to limp into Mrs. Norwood's tiny parlor, which smelled as did the rest of the house of cinnamon buns and oilcloth and camphor.

While her hostess was making tea ("No, no," shrilly, "it's no trouble at all. Why almost every day Mark and I have tea together, don't we, Mark?"), Oriane found that wherever you looked there was something interesting to see—vases and statuettes, framed photographs, little cloisonné boxes, crystal balls; there was a life-size iron dog guarding the coat tree in the hall and three frames of real butterflies in a cabinet opposite her. In fact there were so many things in the parlor that when Mrs. Norwood returned with the tea tray, little Mark preceded her in order to clear a path for her by moving various chairs and small tables out of her way. Glass-fronted bookcases occupied two sides, these filled with dusty, leather-bound volumes, mostly theological tracts together with some sets of the standard classics, none of them had been touched for years, but they gave the room, as Mrs. Norwood would later remark, "a very cozy and cultured look."

However, what Oriane was looking for and in vain was the telephone, and it took her some time to realize that the Norwoods didn't have one at all, especially as her hostess preferred not to tell her so, merely parrying her requests to use the phone by urging her to have some more tea or another cinnamon bun, or repeating that Clayton would be happy to drive her home when he came in.

And before Oriane could insist, that redoubtable lady would be chattering on, perhaps about the china, "My dear, if I'd known that you would honor our poor and humble hearth with your presence, I should have got out the Limoges that belonged to my dear Grandmother Springer. In some ways I preferred her English bone." (She managed by an odd inflection of her voice to imply that the bones of Englishmen were ground up in the porcelain.) "My Grandmother Springer had such a lovely set of English bone but it went to my Aunt Ruth and I don't know what became of it. My Aunt Ruth, you know, went to live in Peoria, Illinois, where she had to undergo many, many vicissitudes. Ah yes," she sighed heavily, and crooking her little finger very daintily, Mrs. Norwood thriftily gathered together the crumbs on her plate with her moistened thumb and popped them into her mouth. Then she helped herself to another cinnamon bun.

"Dear yes," Mrs. Norwood resumed, "many of our family have indeed fallen upon evil times. But I must declare that we are a great deal more fortunate than many. Yes, there are many, many who are much more unfortunate than ourselves."

But the poor and dispossessed never figured long in Mrs. Norwood's conversation, which invariably returned to the grandeurs of Grandmother Springer. At which time her eyes glittered and a strange hypnotic quality invaded her voice—just so must the oracle at ancient Delphi, half suffocated with sulphur fumes, have spoken of her visions—and Oriane, who had small appetite for vanished damasks and brocades and crystal chandeliers, found her attention wandering back to the boy, who, she discovered, was drinking in his mother's words with all the fervor of a true believer.

Poor child, she thought, it's this that gives him the air of a Bonnie Prince Charlie, little realizing that by the rather far-fetched metaphor she had fatally managed to invest the handsome little boy with the romantic glamour that the Young Pretender had always held in her mind, as if his being her young Lochinvar and infant St. George weren't more than enough already.

So while Mrs. Norwood maundered on about the fifteen-foot windows in her grandmother's parlor that boasted lace curtains as well as red velvet drapes, secured with great silk ropes threaded with real gold, Oriane retired into the private pleasure of recollecting the pressure of little Mark's arm about her waist, holding her so tightly as he helped her up the sloping path, and the feel of his thin shoulder under her hand.

Suddenly the room seemed hot and stifling, and dark —either from parsimony or her kookie refinement, Mrs. Norwood never turned on her lights till the last possible moment and kept her curtains drawn against the dying day. As Oriane in her distress and absence of mind shifted in her chair, a pain like fire swept up her leg. A wild, illicit pleasure shot through her at that instant as the sensation of that embrace, so innocent, so chaste, casual, necessary even, stored up it would seem in the very nerves of her hip that had felt his ribs pressed against her, of her thigh that only now released its impression of his belt buckle or something hard in his pocket, a jackknife, perhaps, or a top or a stone—boys always have something hard in their pockets. . . . Oh my God, she said, with revulsion and despair, what am I?

"You had to ring one of those pull-out brass doorbells," Mrs. Norwood was going inexorably on. "You couldn't hear it ring from outside, but presently Maria would come to the door. She always wore the whitest and laciest apron and cap that you ever saw. Once when one of her aprons had a little mended tear in it, my Grandmother Springer made her change it."

Oriane set herself to drinking her tea that was stone cold, she even took half of a cinnamon bun. He is a little boy, she kept telling herself, a little boy, a little boy . . . anyway no one will ever have to know. She glanced over at him now as if to assure herself of his childishness. But to her surprise he was no longer hanging upon his mother's every word as though his life depended on it as he had only a few moments before. Instead he was staring at Oriane, looking at her fixedly out of wide-set, dark eyes, the straight unwavering gaze that children have, comprehending not in the sense of understanding or knowing, but in the complete perception, a visual embrace and absorption of what is looked upon, taken in whole, unclassified and unrelated. And at that moment she experienced once more that kind of thrilling distress that was at once ecstasy and a tearless sorrowing, prevenient and premature, soon gone as she grasped frantically at straws—he does not, cannot possibly, know what he is looking at.

But as far as he was concerned, he seemed to know perfectly well, and when he had caught her eye, he smiled faintly, then with a conjurer's flourish he drew back the curtain at the window beside his chair revealing to her distracted gaze a view of the valley.

It was a pretty one that she had often seen, though from the opposite side; it took in the whole sweep of the little hollow, the light wild grass directly below the Norwoods' house disappeared into brush as the slope deepened and merged into the heavier woods that grew in the bottom; half the shining pond, part of the creek, then above it the white trunks of the birch trees whose frail, trembling leaves made a delicate screen for the lower part of the lawn that in turn ascended the farther and higher hill crowned with the trees sheltering her own house.

But her own house that he showed her now was suddenly transformed. From this vantage, the setting sun fired its windows—even the ones that were sunken behind the trees flashed with light—it became a queer, enchanted citadel: the hill had never seemed so lofty or the house so remote and exalted.

Now there was a great racketing and roaring of a motor outside, wheels squelched on gravel, brakes squealed, a horn blew but apparently inadvertently and a huge old brown Pontiac rocked into the back yard below the window dimming the view with a roiled-up fog of dust and oily smoke.

"Clayton is here," Mrs. Norwood shouted triumphantly over the noise. "In a minute, my dear, he will take you home."

7

The other day a friend of ours, Libby Blaine, called up. Libby works for the local newspaper, *Town Topics,* and she takes a professional interest in all news, whether it's fit to print or not. News in the latter category she handles by spending a very pleasant morning calling up all her friends. So on this morning when I picked up the phone, I heard Libby's rather grating, boyish voice come over the wire. "Sigrid, how's Steve, how's Alison, have you heard the latest?"

"The latest? I doubt it."

"About Giles, I mean. He's got a girl friend."

"Oh?"

"A girl named Sophie Berger. She works in the business office here, of all things. Nice-enough girl. Divorced, not once but twice, through no fault of her own, they say. Anyway, two wedding bands still adorn that fourth finger left hand. She'd be fine for Giles though." Libby gave her short, barking laugh, she had always found Giles unusually hard to take.

"I don't think anybody could be more different from Oriane. Not that that makes any difference, I don't suppose. Oh, she does knit. They do have that in common. Remember how Oriane used to knit all the time? Well this girl's the same way."

"Yes, I remember Oriane's knitting."

"Well, I won't keep you now. You'll be wanting to get back to your writing. Say, when is your book coming out? Tell Steve hello. I'll see you around."

I came away from the phone thinking again, yes, I remember Oriane's knitting. I hadn't thought of it for a long while, but now it seemed if I closed my eyes I could see her there with a pile of wool in her lap and the light glinting off the needles and their nervous click-clicking would punctuate everything she said.

So, Giles has a girl, I thought, but this present information had no reality to compare with the remembered reality of those knitting needles. I was thinking of something that happened years ago, I think it was the first winter we spent in Princeton, in January. We had visited back and forth a certain amount, but I still didn't feel that I knew Oriane very well. I remember thinking that on that winter evening when I went there and Oriane learned that her mother had died.

Confusion is always a concomitant of sudden death; in this case it was complete since the poor lady—her name was Arabel Hathaway, I found out then for the first time—had suffered a heart attack in the subway in New York. She was on the East Side line of the IRT when she was overcome. She managed apparently to revive enough to struggle out of the train at Spring Street, but then she collapsed again. The first person to come to her assistance—though she was probably beyond assistance by then—took her purse, and so for several days the authorities had no way of identifying her. Of course, eventually she was reported missing. Meanwhile Oriane, who lived some fifty miles away, had no reason to believe that anything was wrong, especially since there were always plenty of reasons for her mother not to be in when she telephoned.

So in a weird way Mrs. Hathaway continued for a time to be alive to all those who knew or cared for her, while simultaneously she was a nameless corpse to a conscientious group of strangers, who, it seems, placed her first mistakenly in an ambulance for others to put in a hearse and send to the morgue.

At the end of this long process Steve and I got involved, that is to say Steve volunteered to drive Giles to New York City to identify the body while I stayed with Oriane. Whoever was in charge apparently preferred to deal with the son-in-law and Steve happened to be the first person Giles saw after hearing the news. They decided to keep as much as they could from Oriane until they were sure.

I remember it was in the evening past suppertime when I drove out to Spook Hollow and knocked at the door. Terrified, I remember my feeling that I was the last person in the world for such a mission and I had only the vaguest idea of what had happened and none at all as to how much Oriane knew or how she would act.

And I felt impertinent, I, who hardly knew the daughter, who had never known the mother or had even heard her spoken of, coming to commiserate, or was my sudden appearance going to furnish the final clue that Oriane needed to conclude that something was wrong? The Oriane who kept me waiting for some minutes before she opened the door, and greeted me coolly but without surprise, gave me no inkling. She did ask me to come in and sit down, probably she offered me coffee and I accepted, at all events I remember sitting there and drinking coffee. I remember also that after a while she removed the coffee things and we continued sitting. We didn't talk much, of course.

No, we merely sat together. She on the couch and I on the chair in front of the absolutely clean fireplace. In anyone else's house so clean a hearth meant that it was never used, in Oriane's it meant that after every fire she swept it out.

I looked around that long, low room; its proportions and its oddly placed windows were testimony that it had once been two rooms, and the curious jumble of furnishings—blond modern coffee tables placed in front of the cretonne-covered wing chair and the intricately designed Victorian settee, a little rosewood desk covered over with swirling carved-wood foliage stood uneasily under a Museum of Modern Art reproduction of a Mondrian, a large majolica urn shared the mantelpiece with two Swedish glass vases. I could multiply the examples many times over but the point is not that a mixture of styles and periods is bad in itself, rather in this room the particular combinations clashed with a kind of spiteful bitterness, an incarnation of hurtful, intimate squabblings. On top of the bookcases were little ceramic figures that Oriane had made herself, they were curious, grotesque, competent and primitive. She liked to say, "I wonder what Freud would have made of them."

I looked at the shining winter darkness against the windows, I looked at the ceiling and I looked at the floor, and everywhere, for I found it hard to look at Oriane, who sat stiff and graven-faced upon the couch, but not quite still, fantastically her fingers moved and two glittering red plastic needles darted between them. She was knitting; she knitted so well that she didn't even have to watch what she was doing, sat knitting while we waited. I'm not even sure what we were waiting for, news, I suppose, possibly, after all, there was some uncertainty as to the dead woman's identity, though only a frantic and despairing hope might cling to that uncertainty. Knitting, eyelessly, she sat with that single expression frozen on her face, neither of sorrow, nor hopelessness, but calm, smooth serenity and blank placidity.

Strange, unnatural, I realize now what I did not realize then, I had never before seen her face in repose, it frowned, it laughed, it sneered, it wept, its eyes and mouth were never still, or the brows or chin, a face full of lights and shadows as a racing brook, so that it was hard to call it either handsome or unhandsome, always forming and re-forming, but ugly now in its stillness. Then I realized that she was watching me with the fixed, depthless stare of an African mask. When I looked at her later her lids were drawn down leaving only the frantic knitting hands to betray her—no, not betray, the reverse, to speak for her, express, even lie for her, eloquent to the point of garrulity, and thus reinforce and emphasize the hideous calm with which she waited word of her mother's death.

I thought of Steve, his voice on the telephone had been queer and agitated, Giles, he said, had broken down completely and was crying like a baby. I could imagine that easily enough, sweet, kindly Mr. Chips with his steel-rimmed eyeglasses misted up and tears glistening incongruously on his dusty suit. I sat with the iron-faced maiden, the daughter. *She* might have gone on this hideous errand. . . . It would have been less hard for *her*. I could imagine her saying quite crisply, "Yes, I'll go. Certainly, I'll go."

I was being unfair to Oriane, of course, the silence and the waiting and the quiet were getting on my nerves. And also as the evening wore on it became increasingly impossible for me to believe that she did not know as much as I did. I would tell myself that of course she had not been told anything as yet and then, promptly forgetting that, I would put down her silence and calmness as evidence of an unnatural reserve that must eventually break down, that there would be a violent and terrifying eruption of feeling and emotion with which I could not possibly cope. I felt like a willow shoot, a blade of grass pressed into service to support an oak.

The telephone did ring at last and Oriane got up to answer it and now I heard the clear, cool, precise tones that I had already imagined. "Yes, yes . . . oh, I see . . . yes . . . of course . . . very well . . . yes, that'll be all right . . . good . . . yes . . . yes, she is here . . . well, later, yes . . ." I could see her in profile at the far end of the room standing with the receiver held to her ear, the expression on her face was merely that of waiting till the other one on the line had nothing more to say. "Yes . . . well . . . yes . . . I see . . . later . . . good-bye." Hung up gently.

Returned from the far end of the room to stand in the middle of the carpet in front of the hearth. From looking at her I never would have known that it was not some casual acquaintance who had called with some trifling news, a fellow member of the P.-T.A. telling her the date of a future meeting, for example. She looked at the ash tray on the table beside my chair as though she thought to empty it, a commonplace glance to see that her guest was quite comfortable. Then she told me, "That was Giles. He was calling from New York. My mother is dead."

I must have answered something, but what I remember is her standing before me, her hands crossed over her chest, they looked very white and long and narrow as two lily buds, then she was saying gently and absently, ". . . yes . . . yes . . ." She was looking over me and I saw her shake her head slightly, but for a long moment it did not occur to me that this was meant for someone standing behind me in the doorway. When I finally did turn, I caught only the most fleeting glimpse of Mark Norwood.

But before I could recover from my astonishment, Oriane had begun speaking again. "My God, of course, that's why you came here. You knew she was dead. . . . Oh, she's been dead for days and days. . . . Giles said Steve was with him. . . . Of course, you knew about it!"

"I—I—mean, I thought . . ."

"Oh God, what I was thinking."

She sat down on the couch, suddenly so pale and motionless that I thought she must be faint, then her hand went out, unsteadily, heavily, and picked up the knitting, put it in her lap, folded over it, stiff and mute.

"Oriane, let me get you something."

"Of course it's . . ." she mumbled, so I could make nothing of what she was trying to say.

"I'll get you a drink of water. I'll be right back, Oriane."

She looked at me crazily out of the side of her eyes. "No, never mind. . . . Well, tell Mark to fix me a drink. To fix you one too." This so casually that she might have been speaking of some member of the family, or a servant perhaps, and thus even in her extremity managing in one bold stroke to hide the obvious by focusing it too close for my vision. Once I got out of the living room, Mark was nowhere to be seen, so I nervously rustled about in the cupboards and cabinets till I found the glasses and her liquor closet. When I returned with a glass of brandy for her, Oriane had left the couch for the window seat where she knelt with her face pressed against the panes, a long, soft string of red worsted stretched across to the ball of yarn that had rolled under the coffee table. You couldn't miss it, it showed up like a slash across that fawn-colored carpet. Then I made out the click-clicking of the knitting needles. That fantastic woman had actually gone back to her knitting and purling.

"Here is some brandy, Oriane." I leaned over those rigidly unmoving shoulders and placed the glass on the window ledge, at the same time I caught sight of those flashing needles and the yarn twisted curling around those long white fingers. I retreated at once to the other side of the room. I was covered with confusion, as if I had seen something shocking and shameful. In actual fact, I probably had, but my conscious mind refused to recognize it. Finally, I observed, Oriane reached out and took the glass.

Fifteen, twenty minutes, perhaps a half hour passed, then Oriane stood up. A great sigh escaped her. "You poor darling. Don't cry, please don't." For my eyes had filled with tears. She came toward me, but one heel caught in the spilled yarn and she had to bend down to free it. "It was kind of you to come, it truly was. I really appreciate it very much." The little dry phrases dropped from her like leaves from a tree. Before I knew what she was doing she had taken my arm and had steered me to the hall closet and was helping me on with my coat. "Of course, it's a great shock. What a dreadful way for her to die. But perhaps she didn't realize what was happening. We never can know, of course, what people are thinking at that point. My mother was a wonderful person. I can't believe really . . . Well, I won't think about it now. I'm going to go and lie down for a while. I shall want some rest before Giles comes home. But you were kind to stay so that I wasn't alone when the news came. I'm all right now. Thank you, thank you so much."

She had put on her own coat and walked me to the car. Now she stood there beside it while I warmed up the engine.

"Do go back in the house, Oriane, you'll get cold."

She put her hand on the car door, and I could see the dark streaks across it of the knitting wool still wound about her fingers. "You'll get cold," I repeated.

"Cold?"

"It's very cold."

"Yes, I suppose it is."

"Good-bye, Oriane, I'll call you soon. Do go in the house now."

"Yes, I suppose I am cold."

But she remained there even after I had driven off, I could see her in the rearview mirror, a dark upright shadow in front of the floodlit terrace, with her head bowed as she stared at her yarn-covered hands.

8

"Mark Norwood, you haven't said a word all afternoon, but you're nice to look at anyway."

That was long ago. That was a lifetime ago, that was before the beginning of memory. Rather that was at the moment that memory began. Or should it be called consciousness, that beginning, that stirring of awareness that separates this person from all the others that happen to bear this single name, that happen to occupy this single body, so that no one was aware of this birth, certainly not Oriane herself moving among her guests, that Saturday afternoon in June. Eleven months and a week have passed, that is not really so long, but memory plays such tricks, the stream that is wide would have us believe that it is deep as well, the deception works and the far side is all mistiness and grayness, alien, unattainable region.

"Mark Norwood, you haven't said a word." Be warned, Oriane, be warned.

She was as deaf as any stone. Mark Norwood—he had been away for a little more than two years, of course he had been away at college for four years before that, but she had seen him occasionally during vacations, in a manner of speaking she had kept track of him then, keeping track of the changes in him so she hadn't expected the last two years to change him so much. He had changed enormously. Or perhaps it was she who had changed the moment before. There was simply no time to go into that question now. The good hostess merely catches these things out of the corner of her eye while she talks to Eveline Coughlin about the walking trip she (Mrs. Coughlin) had taken on Cape Cod in 1937.

"Nobody ever walks nowadays and I think it's a shame," that lady had just remarked.

About a yard away, Edna Trotter was telling Mrs. Greene that "Dr. Wilde always takes it personally when one of his patients dies."

Distractedly, Oriane told herself that she must remember to thank Jarry again for the little bottle of homemade pickles.

It was Tessa, of course, clear on the other side of the room, who was blushing. Whether for Mark or for Jarry, it's impossible to say. However, Oriane, who is remarking to Eveline, yes, she doesn't seem to walk as much as she used to, and yes, she is sorry about it, has intercepted the mighty, silent colloquy between Mark and Tessa—ah yes, two years had made a difference there.

Tessa had grown remarkably pretty, with thick red-blond hair and a tall, strong figure. She was slender with long, delicate hands and feet. Of her face with its vivid, dark eyes, Oriane liked to say it had good bones, thus in one stunning blow turning away our compliments and focusing our poor non-X-ray eyes on the fresh loveliness that hid those excellent zygomatic, sphenoid, maxilla and mandible structures. However that may be, Tessa, her eyes brightened by her blushes, arched her brows and smiled almost imperceptibly, then turned her head in a gesture that was at once wonderfully graceful and rather stagy. A moment later Oriane was wishing fretfully that Tessa would fetch some more cake. She had been told time and again that keeping the cake dish filled was her responsibility.

"Mark Norwood . . . you're nice to look at anyway," Jarry Holt had said. Oriane could certainly see that for herself, anyone could, Tessa had, of course.

Mark had smiled uneasily and his face which was quite sun-tanned darkened and he looked even handsomer. The California sun had given him that tan, he'd been at Berkeley studying for his Ph.D. Soon he'd be going to Germany on a Fulbright to work on his thesis. Mrs. Norwood had told all this to everyone in the room any number of times, always adding with a little sniff that she wouldn't dream of keeping him home because his father had recently suffered a stroke, though, of course, it would be a comfort to have him nearer at a time like this.

Before Mark could answer Jarry Holt, she had passed

on to tell Giles (who certainly didn't have to be told) that "This just a cup of coffee business in the morning is a big mistake. That way you start the day with two strikes against you."

"I don't see how you can expect to see anything going by at fifty miles an hour," Eveline Coughlin was saying.

"No, of course not," Oriane managed to agree. Meanwhile, Edna Trotter had remarked that "Dr. Wilde was sad for days and days when old Mrs. Campbell died. But, of course there was nothing he could do about it."

Giles would be perverse. "Still, the French are supposed to know more about food than anyone else on earth and all they ever have in the morning is coffee and a crouton."

Croissant for God's sake, thought Oriane in dismay.

"That's exactly what's the matter with the French," Jarry crowed with triumph. "Look what happened to them in the war. No breakfast and no backbone."

"Why, when we were going to Dennis we sat down for a while near the road and we saw a sea gull with only one leg."

"All I want to say is that I've read that people with a tendency to arteriosclerosis aren't supposed to eat eggs because the fat in the albumen coats their veins and makes them crack."

Oriane turned her head to look out of the window with despairing eyes, staring down the rock path edged with pansies and sweet alyssum; the grass beyond was lush and inviting. She looked past the gracefully knotted trunk of the Chinese dogwood, its myriad white blossoms lay on its new green leaves like anomalous snow. Her gaze wandered down to where the path divided; one side lost itself behind a slope in the ground, the other wound away into the meadow and the woods that lay beyond the garden. She had a sense of a close stillness in the nature of that long shadowed afternoon, suspended and waiting for everything and nothing, waiting for Jarry to say "One doesn't have to eat *eggs* for breakfast," waiting for Tessa to remember to fetch the other cake, waiting for the party to be over, for Mark Norwood to speak, for her own mood to change, waiting as one awaits a storm or a crisis and seeing nothing beyond.

Mrs. Dingman poked her fork into the cake and lifted a too large piece to her mouth, a bit of the frosting stuck on her lip. Oriane could see it though she quickly turned her face away and fixed her eyes on the nothingness of the sky, suddenly cut by the flight of a single bird, black and small and quick as a shadow in an arc between the trees. Looking and not seeing, hearing and not listening, while the others talked, ah why did they chatter so filling the air with gentle twittering of polite, ladylike voices like a company of crickets.

Then she started out of it a little guiltily and felt that Professor Thurby had touched her arm, saw his eyes on her, strangely pale and vacant as the sky, gently playing over her face, caressing, exploring, noting, Oriane dreams, said the dreamy eyes. Oriane smiled.

He smiled back but before he could speak, Oriane heard a little whispery voice in her ear saying, "Why, hello Oriane darling." Oriane looked down into a dark, nervously ticking face that was mounted over a bust of tinkling glass beads. It was Patricia Crory, the younger of two spinsters who lived all by themselves in a huge, spooky Victorian house built by their grandpapa. They saved everything, hats, shoes, newspapers, string, dresses, beads, ribbons, buttons, dance programs, laces, photographs, anything that had any possible use or interest left in it—in fact the only thing they had ever wasted was their lives, ruined in the same way that a fine scarf put away in a chest is ruined, from care and niggardliness and disuse.

"I saw you looking out the window, Oriane."

"Yes, I'm not being a very good hostess, I'm afraid."

"Oh no, no, no," said the other, frightened. "I mean, I think Tessa's looking perfectly beautiful these days."

"Thank you, Patricia."

"You know, I like to think that all of life comes thronging to the door of one and twenty."

"Yes . . ."

Besides the beads, Patricia was wearing a salmon-pink scarf of Indian silk that had undoubtedly belonged to her mother or grandmother—it was covered with little colored puckers, and although it was at least a yard wide and two yards long, it could be passed through a little finger ring. She fiddled with the scarf now, brushing it softly back and forth against her chin.

"When I was one and twenty I wanted to be a singer. . . . It's funny when you think of all the things that might have been but aren't." She was so earnest that she had twisted one end of the Indian scarf around her arm. "Sister says when I talk that way, it's silly. I suppose I don't express myself very well." Now she looked down on the twisted scarf and sighed.

"I think Mark Norwood is so interesting," she said presently.

"Really? What did you talk about?"

"Oh, I didn't talk to him. But I think his face is fascinating." She puckered up her own wistfully, then she smiled and opened her innocent brown eyes very wide. "I think it would be the most romantic thing if he and Tessa got together. I mean, they would make such a handsome couple."

Oriane writhed inwardly; scratch any old maid and you will find a matchmaker.

"Yes, I suppose so." Oriane noticed again that the cake dish was practically empty and glanced reproachfully at Tessa who was standing around as still and idle as a folded-up umbrella. "Excuse me a minute, Patricia." She took up the cake plate and marched righteously over to her daughter with it, not even diverted by Ida Dingman who automatically reached out with her fork and slid the last crumbly piece of cake off the serving dish onto her own. "Waste not, want not," she said cheerily. "Oriane, you simply must give me the recipe."

"Yes," Oriane answered coldly, then thrust the empty dish into Tessa's hands. "If you don't *mind*, dear." She had spoken more sharply than she had intended, now she bit her lip.

Off to her right, Mrs. Norwood was saying, "Why, nobody can tell me that people weren't happier fifty or seventy-five years ago than they are now. In those days they had *values*."

Directly in front of her Jarry was shouting that a good old-fashioned porridge is good, gives you some ballast for the day.

Oriane looked out the window once more at the path that wound down the hill. *Mark Norwood, you haven't said a word all afternoon,* Jarry had said. But who could get a word in edgewise into the solid pack of middle-aged lady chatter that filled the room?

Suddenly it flashed through Oriane's mind that if it were only night she would go and take Mark by the hand and lead him through the French windows. She would kick off her shoes and run with him down the hill to the Hollow.

She turned and looked dreamily around the room. How long would it take them to notice that she was gone? Quite a while, no doubt, but eventually they would. Some of them would sneak out into the kitchen looking for her, others might go upstairs, and they would be vaguely uneasy, milling around waiting for a leader to show them what to do. Then they would start to go, all of them giving messages to Giles, tell Oriane it's been lovely. "Yes," he would say blankly, having no idea why they didn't tell her themselves.

Oriane would never be able to say afterward how long this dream went on. All she would remember was that suddenly the room was filled with the hubbub of people saying good-bye.

Jarry was pumping her arm up and down. "Oriane darling, I've had a wonderful time. Your hands are cold."

"Warm heart," said Oriane.

"Ummm. Ida Dingman," Jarry said without pausing, "you're coming with me? Anyone else want a lift? Well. All right. Winifred, I'm so sorry I didn't have a chance to speak to you. Trouble with these big affairs, you mostly talk to who you're talking to. Do give me a ring at the Y, I'm sure we'll find somebody to cut your lawn. Tessa darling, you will come to our dance next month. I have a love of a boy for you. He's from Montreal and he's studying to be a licensed pharmacist . . ."

She kissed Tessa and stared at her for a second,

suddenly dropped her voice into a conspirator's whisper. "Take care of yourself, child."

Ida managed to make off with still another piece of cake from the refilled platter. She gobbled it down in three bites in order to be ready to go with Jarry. "I think this is the most delicious cake that I've ever eaten. Oriane, you simply must give me the recipe for it."

"Yes, Ida, yes, of course."

Now it was Beatrice Norwood who was saying good-bye. A hectic flush had stained her usually pale and pasty features and she kept nodding her head without any reason except that she had somehow to express her animation. Also, she appeared a little angry that Jarry had beaten her out of the queen's prerogative of leaving first and now, though she desperately wanted to stay, she also wanted to be the second to leave.

Reluctance made her draw out her farewells fantastically. "Oriane darling, it's been so lovely, I hate to leave, but poor Clayton, you know, of course he sleeps most of the time, he is so frail, so very, very frail. But dear, I wanted to tell you there's no one who knows how to entertain people so royally. I mean that dear . . ." She was making a regular speech and Oriane found herself looking beyond her at Tessa and Mark who were whispering and laughing together. Perhaps she felt her mother's eyes upon her, because Tessa looked up and smiled.

"And the cake was magnificent. May I ask a little favor? May I take a little teensy slice home to Clayton? He would enjoy it, I know." With that, she scooped up the rest of the cake in a paper napkin while babbling on, "I didn't tell you Mark was coming because I thought it would be such a nice surprise, and I will speak for him, he's enjoyed every minute of it, I'm sure."

"Okay, Tessa, I'll pick you up around eight," Oriane distinctly heard Mark say.

Through the window, Oriane could see Jarry Holt maneuvering her battered blue Rambler skittishly out the drive, narrowly missing the copper beech, caroming into the yielding wall of rhododendrons on the other side, oh well, no damage done, a few leaves and twigs torn off; one could fairly imagine Jarry Holt saying "oh damn" and then keep right on driving, turning directly into the road without the slightest pause to watch the traffic; there was a screech of brakes—another car's—and Jarry was safely under way.

"That'd be super," said Tessa, "but make it eight-thirty."

Then Libby Blaine was saying "Good-bye, Oriane," and Sigrid, and dear old Ed Thurby saying something arch and gallant, then Edna and Patricia and Estella, all of them saying good-bye, dear, good-bye, Oriane. Then all by herself she was walking back into the living room, without even realizing what she was doing, she went to the philodendron plant on the table and began to strip off the not-quite-perfect leaves and tuck them into the earth in the pot.

But already the little incident is repeating itself in her mind. Jarry Holt kissing Tessa dryly on the cheek. "Take care of yourself, child."

Why did she say that?

It's not important. Think of all the other things she says.

"Take care of yourself, child." Mouth pursed up, round button eyes staring into the girl's face.

"Yes, Mrs. Holt."

How can you tell the difference between a wise old woman and a silly old woman, they all give you advice and the lines around their eyes make them look shrewd, and besides, one has been taught to defer and listen, my child, to the gabby voice of experience.

The mind is a book with a broken spine so that it always falls open to the same page. Without warning, without reason, Oriane will recollect the little scene, even after everything has changed so utterly and completely that she can no longer even relate the present to that past.

Afterward, three months afterward, say, Tess, Mark and Oriane have all driven out to the airport together. They were early, after all, getting there and while they waited they had gone into the restaurant. "Have your last cup of good American coffee," the waiter said heavily. Oriane ordered it, but once it was there, she didn't want to drink it.

The soothing, ubiquitous, almost subliminal music broadcast through the building made her want to scream. "Of course I know there's only one crash to so many millions of passenger miles," Oriane said glumly. "But statistics like that never reassure me very much."

She lifted the cup to her lips but still didn't drink it. Now she had noticed that Mark had ordered himself a complete meal. Tomato juice, filet of sole, French fries, rolls—the poor boy probably had been too nervous to eat before. Now she watched in fascination as he took up the roll, broke it, then with his knife scooped up a little butter from the soft square pat on its little round of cardboard.

"Considering everything, though, I suppose I'm actually as brave as a lion."

Now she watched the butter-laden knife rub itself

against the waiting piece of roll, then her glance shifted to the hand that held it. Long fingers, prominent knuckles, the faintest gleam from thin, long hairs on the backs of his fingers, the skin on the knuckles was loose and somewhat reddened.

Then for no reason at all, *Mark Norwood, you haven't said a word all afternoon, but you're nice to look at anyway.*

She is between sleeping and waking in that big, dim hotel room in Friani. Streaks of white light penetrate the iron blind at the window, it bangs and rattles as the swallows swoop in and out of their nests with marvelous, careless proficiency. The metallic clanking and the harsh, shrill racketing of the nestlings have probably awakened her; contrasting sharply with the glacial stillness within the room. That dreamless beloved at her side sleeps as quietly as a child. It is cold and too early for her to think of getting up, she slips her hands under his body thrilled with the sudden radiant warmth that courses up from the palms of her hands to the most secret parts of her body. Eyes closed, almost asleep again, Jarry Holt's voice rings in her ears, it's loud and brisk, it's a kindly and no-nonsense voice that would never let tact tamper with frankness. *Take care of yourself, child.*

Oriane is walking down a street in Rome. She has a package under one arm containing the charming hand-embroidered blouse that she has just bought in the little shop on the Via Veneto. It was certainly no bargain, but the moment that she had caught sight of it in the window she had known that she would have to have it. Her other arm rests lightly on Ed Thurby's—that sweet professor who had blushed so and puffed so hard when they met quite unexpectedly a few minutes before.

Oriane hadn't remembered he was in Europe and now she was strangely touched at seeing him again.

"I envy you, my dear, really settling down in that little town in Tuscany. What is its name again?"

But before she can answer, the present has vanished from her mind and in its stead she is standing in her living room at Spook Hollow looking across the group of friends. Jarry Holt's gray head suddenly eclipses Tessa's red-and-gold as she kisses the girl's cheek.

The young man, head and shoulders taller than any of them, with a fine dark head and princely features, when he smiled his teeth looked as white as an Indian's; the expression in his eyes, startled and embarrassed, more than that, a kind of burning hotness, then an instant shadow, oh she had imagined it, and a moment later the long curling lashes swept downward, hiding and curtaining, when he looked up his eyes were as empty as glass.

Then telescoped by memory's cunning selection, immediately and without transition, Oriane would feel her hand grasped firmly, almost roughly, by Jarry Holt; those dry lips would brush against her cheek. Jarry had uttered her swift warning, a conventional phrase, ambiguous caution. The lips almost white and still pursed up from the kiss, popping eyes blue as china, flopping gray bangs, the Dutch-boy haircut she had adopted a good forty years earlier in her woman suffrage days, a shapeless tweed suit on a bulldog-square body. Perhaps Jarry merely had an eye for opposites. Herself, she couldn't keep quiet any more than a teakettle.

She steamed away. "Come on, Ida, no more chitchat. I'll be calling you, Libby, about the bureau. I should think somebody could use it. It's a perfectly good bureau, drawers work, all that sort of thing, quite absurdly ugly, hide it in a closet. Well, good-bye, Oriane, it's been like old times. Your roses ought to be cut back. Meant to mention it before. I noticed it when I came in. Oh, about those pickles, you may not like them. It's a recipe from the Poconos, the alum water makes them bitter. You ready, Ida? You're waiting for me? Well, we're off then. Lovely, lovely, good-bye everybody. I have to drop by at the A & P first, that's all right with you, Ida? It won't take a minute. I want to get some coffee, perfectly good in bags. Where's my other glove? I haven't lost it again! Oh, here it is in my pocket. And here's a key. I found it on my desk the other day. I haven't the faintest idea what it's for. Good-bye again everybody. If I don't stop talking I'll never get any-where. My mother used to say if I got a penny a word I'd be as rich as John D. Rockefeller within a month."

Go softly now, Oriane, into that past, tread slowly and pick your way carefully in those tortuous lanes, the less to disturb those memories, frail and damp and becom-ing earth like last year's leaves, suspend your subsequent memories lest miracles and prodigies invade that quiet scene, soothsayers and augurs stand at every hand with ready prophecies and every star and bird in flight gives sign and signal of what is to come.

Merely, it is Jarry Holt going off into the peaceful afternoon. June's long shadows lie on the grass but there is a hint of an earlier season's coldness in the blue-hued air. She'd made a snap judgment as easily and naturally as a squirrel flirts his tail, and it meant no more to her. Quite possibly she hadn't meant to judge at all, the turn of words formed of themselves—the facile coinage that bears no stamp of the mind is spent without thought.

9

"From the terrace I can look for miles and miles over the countryside. We are on the top of a mountain here, and the land slopes away quite steeply outside the walls, but just the same every inch is cultivated, planted with vineyards and olive groves. Some of the olive trees must be a thousand years old, their trunks are all rotted and hollowed out and the only thing that attaches them to the ground is a little skin of bark.

"The peasants have big white oxen to pull their plows, I can't tell you how beautiful these beasts are with their big soulful brown eyes and black eyelashes about an inch long. Way off in the distance there's a ruined castle. I mean to visit it one day because it looks very romantic. Belonged to Frederick Barbarossa or some such spook, but it's hard to get to and we're told there's nothing special inside.

"Of course you can't find Friani on your map. Good old Baedeker found it and here's what he has to say about it, quote: ' (1043 ft) , an ancient and loftily situated town with 2738 inhab, was a prosperous and independent place in the 13th and 14th cent, but in 1357 after having suffered terribly in consequence of an outbreak of the plague that wiped out almost all of its inhabitants, it became subject to Florence. Clumsily restored frescoes in the Museo Civico record the event. Towers and impressive fortifications well preserved; Gothic Cathedral façade modernized in bad taste.' End quote. Frankly I sort of like the cathedral, which shows I'm either more tasteless or more tolerant than old Mr. B., and of course weathering has certainly helped; the stones here turn a beautiful pinkish-gold, like clouds touched by a sunset. Of course, it has the biggest, loudest bell in the world and they ring it about a hundred times a day and every time that happens I swear I'm going to take the first bus out of here.

"Speaking of buses—some bright-eyed bushy tail at the CIAT figured out that the tourist business was just what the town needed. So they put on some special buses three times a week to fetch out the gold-bearing travelers from Florence who help out the café business in the square and buy up the undeniably handmade handiwork of the industrious needlewomen hereabouts. There's a pottery works which the tourist may visit and see curly-headed little children diligently laboring away, there's a school on the premises which is proudly pointed out where the children learn among other

106

things to belt out such appealing chestnuts as 'Santa Lucia' and 'Ciribiribin.' Orders may be shipped anywhere in the world. . . ."

Poor Oriane covers pages and pages with this stuff; writing with a thick-nibbed pen and green ink, slanting, squared-off script, the i's are dotted with a little line and the t's are capped with a big line that never crosses them with the result that to a casual eye everything she writes looks underlined and enthusiastic, an effect that vaguely pleases her. She rereads each letter when she has finished it, almost always adds a P.S. or two in the margins; invariably seals it, addresses it and stamps it before going on to write an almost identical letter to someone else.

She has taken her writing materials in a big Florentine-leather case out to the terrace and sits in a wicker lounge chair sunning herself as she writes; it is hot and still, for everyone in Friani is sensibly indoors eating or taking a siesta in cool, darkened rooms.

"They all think I'm out of my mind, but I'm getting the most gorgeous tan you ever saw in your life. I think when I go down to Rome I'll get myself a yellow dress. There's the most divine shop on the Via Sistina where you can have anything made up in any color or any material you want. I . . ."

In truth, the sun was making her lightheaded. In spite of her dark glasses, her eyes were so dazzled that when she closed them great pinwheels of purple fire seemed to be slowly unwinding against her vision. Everything was hot to her touch, her pen, her paper, the leather case, the wicker chair, her skin. Along the top of the sun-struck stone balustrade, the air visibly rippled and whirligigged from the heat.

She opened her eyes wide and tried to collect herself.

"I think when I go down to Rome, I'll get myself a yellow dress. . . ." To continue the letter she reread the words and thought fuzzily, But when can that be? We haven't even talked of going to Rome. Of course, we won't stay in Friani forever. But what on earth is forever, at this point I can't even think of tomorrow or next week, let alone next year.

With the practiced, automatic hand of the woman who is always anointing herself, Oriane reaches for the plastic bottle of lotion that is beside her chair; her hands unscrew it without the aid of her eyes or even her distracted attention, and begin carefully and methodically to apply the colorless, greaseless, pleasantly scented oil to her face, first to her poor dazzled eyes, removing her dark glasses and rubbing it well into the soft skin beneath them, then her nose and mouth; the hands did not neglect themselves, rubbing themselves together, palm to palm, while the fingers slithered over the backs with the soothing unguent. Her mind was as distant and as vacant as the heat-drowned sky while her hands worked on. There's so much I cannot possibly write in my letters home. They'd get the shock of their lives if I . . . The hands were not finished till she had removed her sandals and they applied the precious emollient to the very soles of her feet. Then the hands capped the bottle securely and returned it to its place beside her chair.

Soothed and renewed by the little rite, Oriane can now continue with her letter writing, spinning around herself the shimmering iridescent web of a specious happiness, larding her descriptions with little anecdotes, how she had ordered grapes inadvertently thinking to order eggs, *uva* instead of *uova*, how she had asked for salt (*sale*) and received a salad (*insalata*); she relates the story of the man in the white coat whom she met on the bus, including the practical jokester from Hartford, dead-pan telling as she wonders if anyone besides herself would find it heartbreaking. Next she'll tell of her encounters with the village idiot, a deaf-mute named Vani, "whom I apparently fascinate."

"Which is really quite delightful at my time of life and of course my Italian is such that I really get along best with an Italian who can't speak at all. Besides, he likes to pick up the cigarette butts I throw away. Doesn't smoke them himself, I don't believe. Too pure or too poor, probably salvages the tobacco and sells it. Has gorgeous blue eyes of all things and he always has a calm, rapt look on his face as though he were listening to celestial voices. Sort of a queer type to have tagging along after you when you step outside for a breath of air."

All of which sounds very straightforward and light-hearted, at least Oriane hopes it does. The reality, of course, is rather more complicated and disturbing. In the first place, Oriane never simply "stepped outside for a breath of air." She made excursions, sorties, if you will, expeditions. The simplest errand became a ritual to be planned and prepared for; her dress, her face, her hair, her hands, feet, all had to be carefully attended to, another woman going to the opera could not be more careful as to the details of her appearance than Oriane going to the square to buy a newspaper.

While she talked, talked, talked, a stream of bright chatter that like her letters pretended to a blitheness that she certainly could not have felt. Sometimes she even prevaricates—certainly as much to herself as to

Mark who is too busy with his own work to pay much attention to what she is saying—such as, "Oh, I must hurry or one of those damn buses will unload a flood of tourists in the plaza."

The little untruth slips off her tongue as smoothly and lightly as constant repetition can make it, for, like many inexperienced travelers, she hopes to appear worldly by avoiding her kind. But for a long while now idleness and the desire to hear other American voices have been driving Oriane out into the streets and plazas during the "rush hour." Alas, she suffers mortally from homesickness but who can name that malaise which she so steadfastly refuses to admit to, when thoughts of home become so inextricably meshed with regrets for the past.

That long, long past like a thick, unwieldy volume, its pages gray, so tightly printed in agate type, a history of blunders and mistakes, murky unclear passages, dull, pedestrian interludes, petty worries, petty disappointments, little ambitions frustrated, little successes proving empty, even the despairs and agonies she had suffered therein lacked magnitude or dignity, herself the author with the power at every juncture to emend and omit, to add, to rewrite, but, no, she had waited till far too late, lingered with an idle pen as all the proofs went in, galley and page, off to the bindery it goes, this sorry stillborn epic that is her life, still life—*nature morte*— away with it, put it aside and step out into the Italian sunlight.

The streets of Friani lack sidewalks and are paved with cobblestones, narrow, steeply sloping, winding seemingly at random till one reflects how easily in any one of them a whole army might be bottled up by a few bowmen on the roofs. It is therefore rather depressing to walk in these mazy alleys where one is ever reminded of battles that never did take place, of a whole population beggaring itself in such an artful and elaborate and fanatical search for complete security while allowing its cellars to be infested with hordes of plague-ridden rats.

Rats which even today remain among the fattest and most prosperous of Friani's inhabitants, chief scavengers, ubiquitous; Oriane at various times has discovered herself to be spied upon from cracks and crevices by various pairs of beady eyes, she has also heard their racketings at night in the walls and ceiling but manages with typical American finickiness to attribute the noises to other causes. To the cats perhaps.

Vicious, unlovely creatures too, for that matter, tough, starving, quite as wild as the rats, their short, violent lives spent in an agelong stalemated battle with the rats, preying on the weaker members of that tribe, just as their own less fit fall victim to the rats, each effecting to produce in the other a superrace of cats and rats, superior in the savage virtues of cunning and hardiness, cruelty, boldness, ferocity, and the prodigious fecundity of the females. Thus we may perhaps smile when we see Oriane all dolled up on her way to the piazza carrying a little package of goodies from her table which she takes up a certain blind alley and calls, "Here kitty, kitty, pretty kitty," to a flea-bitten, dead-eyed, spitting and snarling little member of the clan who probably ounce for ounce is one of the fiercest creatures in the world. Oriane stoops down to spread out her paper and leaves her little offering clean and tempting in the middle of it, but while she lingers it will not be touched. Later, of course, it is gone but we decline to say flatly that it was a cat who got it.

One day as Oriane comes out of the alley she encounters Vani, that deaf-mute whom she has mentioned in her letters home. At first she is startled and frightened, for the place is relatively lonely, but the boy is so poor and small in his pathetic rags and he looks at her so innocently and so wistfully out of those uncomprehending blue eyes of his that her courage returns and she smiles at him as she turns to go.

Instantly his hands go up in the traffic cop's unequivocal sign to stop where she is. Puzzled, Oriane does so, still smiling, and she is rewarded with such a beaming and enraptured look that she waits patiently. Vani's hands fold themselves in a sign of prayer, repeated two or three times and then again they raise themselves, the fingers straight up and the palms turned outwards. Unmistakably he means that he prays that she will stop and stay for a moment. She nods her head and continues smiling.

Now he dashes into the alley where she can hear him rattling about, rustling papers, making other vague, undefined noises. She glances up and down the street. It is not as deserted as she had thought at first. Four or five doors down there's a *salsamenteria,* a tiny, almost invisible establishment that she had overlooked at first, but a woman goes in carrying a straw basket and in a moment another woman comes out with her basket filled. There's an old man sitting on a stoop only a little farther away reading a newspaper, and in the other direction two children are squatting over something they have found in the gutter. From one of the windows above the street comes "Mrs. Brown, You Have a Lovely Daughter" rendered in Italian over a radio that's tuned to its loudest.

Vani has returned bearing a gift. No prince presenting his queen with a priceless gem could exhibit more elegance and pride. He bows low with a flourish. Oriane wishes she might curtsy though he is quite satisfied by her smile. But the gift, she notices with some consternation, is wrapped up in the paper in which she had brought the scraps and tied up with the identical string. However—now she has taken it from him—it is rather heavier than before, in fact quite heavy. His beaming, eager face urges her to open it.

She does so, carefully untying the string, unfolds the paper—there is still a newspaper-wrapped parcel inside, this she unwraps and finds a stone. An ordinary, squared-off, grayish stone, perhaps a cobblestone that had come loose in the street, a stone with any history or none, a stone—merely a stone.

A stone accompanied by that ravishing, radiant look from those rapt blue eyes that seem to gaze on Paradise. Oriane had no idea how she could rise to such a gift—a stone. She smiles and smiles and touches it tentatively—so ordinary a stone is it that it is dusty and dirty and leaves a smudge on her hand. It is out of the question for her to take it with her and yet for a while she hesitates wondering what on earth she should do with it. Finally, however, she folds the wrappings carefully, winds up the string in a figure eight around two fingers, and putting them down on a little building ledge, places the stone carefully on top of them. Then she smiles again at Vani and departs for the square without turning around even once.

On another occasion, perhaps three or four weeks later, Vani has a second gift for her. This time the wrappings—old newspapers, of course—showed signs that the parcel had been prepared quite a while previously.

Not only that but it must have been wrapped and unwrapped many times and also carried around a good deal.

Oriane had continued leaving table scraps in the alley and had even tried to improve the quantity and quality of these offerings as the notion occurred to her that it was Vani and not the cats who needed them, however she never saw him in the alley, or, for that matter, anywhere else, though actually from her arrival in Friani, the poor witless boy followed her almost everywhere.

He had been in the crowd of idlers at the bus depot on that first evening when Oriane had been set down amidst all the bags and boxes brought from Florence. Then, as many times afterward, she was much too busy with her own affairs to perceive that ragged boy, perhaps sixteen years old, with the transfigured idiot's face. Others had rushed forward to take her bags, fetch a taxi, offer themselves as guides and interpreters and all the rest; Vani probably merely tagged along intrigued by the bright, rich stuffs she wore, the exotic (to him) flavor of America that she radiated, and above all attracted to that waxy, doll-like, artificial face, narrowed by the two flat, gleaming wings of hair. The harsh fluorescent lighting of the station blued her hair and likewise the rouge on her cheeks and lips till she resembled some image of Our Lady of Sorrows.

As there was only one hotel in town where she would be likely to stay, even Vani would find it simple to follow her there, and presently a light going on in an upper window overlooking a terrace would be sufficient to inform him of the exact room. His waiting was rewarded by the sight of her coming out and standing in the open for a few minutes as she gazed over the roof-tops; she never once looked down, but if she had she never would have seen him, so deeply hidden was he among the shadows. Then she turned her head as though someone had spoken to her from inside, and after one more glance at the view, she returned to the room.

Thus had begun the endless, mindless, albeit inter-mittent vigil—sometimes Vani forgot and minded his own poor affairs, but then, sooner or later, he would come across her in the street and begin to follow her again. And Oriane never even became aware of his presence until he stepped forth once and once again to give her "gifts," so modest and casual was this shadow.

Friani's park, if we may call it that, actually no more than some carefully tended strips of green lawn and alternate beds of ivy with occasional geraniums and petunias growing in urns, was located atop the old ramparts. Here and there along the promenade, trees such as ilex and umbrella pines that had managed to find a precarious footing outside the walls afforded pleas-ant shady spots. Stone benches, some unobtrusive statues and a small fountain were provided. The views were splendid, both of the deep, picturesque valley below Friani and the mountains beyond, and of the town itself. Here, furthermore, there was almost always a breeze stirring and the gurgling water in the fountain added the illusion of coolness and freshness to the place.

Oriane had found the park quite by accident—in fact she liked to say in this sense she was accident prone, for she always went out without a map or guidebooks. In any case, once she had found the park she returned to it almost daily, even choosing for herself a bench from which the view was particularly fine. Her feeling when she was here was that at last she had come in contact with Italian life, for here there were children playing and old men dozing in the sun and lovers walking two by two. She would buy *gelati* from a white-painted street cart and eating the cold, sweet ice from a waxed envelope feel girlish and carefree. Of course, she was stared at, because the Italians stare and stare, they even stare at one another, and of course she was approached by venders of Parker pens and Swiss watches cheap, and postcards, but she was here so often that the regulars learned to take her for granted.

It was here that Vani came one day to present her with his second gift. The parcel was wrapped, as I have said, in deeply creased newspapers, secured by an incredibly dirty string, perhaps the very one that Oriane had used a good month earlier on the package of table scraps she had left in the alley.

Vani walked, for once, boldly in the middle of the promenade instead of skulking in the shadows in the wake of his beloved. His head was high with pride and even while he was much too far off for her to make out his expression he began to smile. He walked directly up to her and beamed down at her, then with a deep bow he took the parcel from under his arm and presented it to her.

She accepted it, not without some trepidation, it was too light to be another stone; she fumbled with the string, for it was very tightly knotted, but finally she managed by slipping the loop over one end. The ink from the paper smudged her hands, but for once she didn't care. I suppose everybody likes surprises and this would certainly be a surprise, but it was the boy who had touched her with his giving, he was the only person in all of Italy to have given her anything. She regretted that she had not kept the stone. She would keep this, whatever it was, no matter what it was, she would keep it.

It was a pair of wind goggles, the kind that come from the cheapest stores and are worn by the drivers of motor scooters and such; not new, certainly very, very old, lacking glass, every particle of glass had been removed from the frames. These two heavy circles were set in a domino of cracked red plastic dangling a loop of filthy elastic band from which the broken rubber strands protruded like little worms. The thing lay in its bed of rumpled papers reminding her of the decapitated head of a Martian. She would keep it, it was probably the most precious thing he had and he had given it to her.

He was smiling and smiling and she smiled back, wishing with all her heart that she could give him something in exchange, but for once she had come out without her purse and she had no money or even cigarettes in her pockets.

Well, when she met him again, she would be the one with gifts.

"Thank you, thank you so much. It is beautiful. I can't tell you how grateful I am." Even as she was saying the words she knew how foolish it is to speak in English to an Italian deaf-mute, but she couldn't contain herself and said "Thank you" over and over again. She hugged the horrid object too, and even tried it on, peeking at him through the glassless holes.

Finally she wrapped it again in its newspapers, and looped the string about the whole thing. She stood up to leave, holding it in both hands over her breast.

Then to her surprise he took it from her, smiling still, and slipped it back under his arm. The five fingers of his free hand he held to his lips for an instant, kissing them, then he held them up and slowly opened his hand, looking at it all the while and smiling. He beamed at her then and patted the parcel and with a bow suddenly turned and walked abruptly away.

Oriane stood there for a few minutes with her hand over her mouth, pressing and pressing, till she became aware of the odor on it of newspaper and plastic and brassy metal. Then she returned to the hotel.

It is a typical day, not Sunday, midafternoon and Friani is beginning to come to life again after its siesta; the shadows are beginning to cool, soft and velvety with the golden dust that shimmers in the air. A child is screaming somewhere indoors, the shopkeepers are ringing up their iron gates with great clatterings and banging, a radio is on full blast so the whole neighborhood may enjoy it, a skinny dog trots by full of purpose; down the street an ass is bellowing under his master's blows. A small group of Americans go by giving the man black looks for abusing an animal so but they know too little Italian to interfere; the net result, of course, is that the poor creature gets a few extra licks for good measure.

Oriane, whose sense of timing has always been magnificent, arrives in Friani's central plaza just as the clock on the tower of the Signorial Palace begins to strike. Four *carabinieri*, brilliant enough to be in an opera, stalk by with wonderful militaristic clankings and jingling, their heavy metal-reinforced boots striking off sparks on the round, golden cobblestones. The four walk abreast but the third to the left is not quite in step; a great flock of pigeons rise up in front of them in noisy, whistling, mock panic.

The plaza itself is undeniably handsome—a semicircle —the Signorial Palace occupies the straight side while lovingly antique-type buildings close in the outer curve. There are numerous cafés here and many delightful shops to attract the tourists who usually wish to cheer themselves up after a visit to the Museo Civico in the Signorial Palace.

That edifice contains not only the afore-mentioned clumsily restored but extremely graphic frescoes of the plague year, a room full of medieval torture instruments, some arms and armor, a case of poison rings, some nineteenth-century paintings of famous battles; those with good hearts and lungs may ascend one hundred and seventy-two steps to the tower and on the way see the little stone closets in which certain unfortunates were allowed to starve to death within the view of the populace; the outlook from the top, of course, is splendid. On the way out one may see a room devoted to the works of the Master of Friani (doubtless several artists) portraying the martyrdom of the saints. Finally, next to the exit is a little collection of World War II memorabilia—mostly captured German uniforms, flags, small arms, et cetera. The guide calls one's attention to dark stains on one of the helmets and on a bayonet which he explains are dried blood.

So after these tours, which take around half an hour, the tourists fan out very quickly from the steps of the

Signorial Palace into the lovely plaza which seems particularly warm and bright with its Bernini-type fountain splashing clear, sparkling water high in sun-struck air. They make their way to the little shops to buy embroidered linens and blouses or gay painted pottery featuring roosters and flowers; leather goods sometimes appeal, tooled and engraved with elaborate red-and-gold designs, pocketbooks, wallets, writing cases and the like; in these stores English is spoken by pretty, convent-bred young ladies and it occurs to almost no one to haggle about the outrageous prices that are asked.

Usually there is still some time before the bus is scheduled to depart to go to the cafés that are assiduously fitted out with checked red tablecloths and wire-back chairs; a few of the bolder travelers order *caffè espresso*, others merely ask for hot water in which they put a teaspoonful of instant coffee that they providently brought from home. In any case, the *gelati* and *cassata* please or the little frosted cakes with all kinds of fanciful designs.

The American voices are rather loud, but very jolly and good-natured; some of them like to sprinkle their speech with such Italian words as *subito, pronto* and *gabinetto* (this last, they find very amusing); a few of the linguistic geniuses among them can manage *cameriere*, but most of the men like to address the waiter as Giuseppe, hey! Which does well enough.

Oriane has a special café to which she always goes—not by coincidence the largest and most attractive of the lot and therefore the most crowded. Most of its tables and chairs are out-of-doors, of course, on the sidewalk, but they are contained in an area that is enclosed by a little, carefully pruned box hedge set out in white-painted planters. There's a table in a corner by the hedge that Oriane particularly favors as it commands a view of the plaza as well as most of the nearby tables. It is also a little shaded at this time of day by a red-and-white-striped awning and she knows from looking at the other women sitting under it that the rose light it affords is particularly warm and alluring.

She has entered the plaza now in the wake of the marching *carabinieri* and in the company of a lot of skipping and shouting little boys who are very excited and inspired by the sight, the pigeons are wheeling overhead in a great flapping, whistling flock leaving their shadows to dance on the stones below. Both enchanted and apprehensive, Oriane walked quickly through these circling shadows just as the last notes from the striking clock were dying away. "It would be just my luck," she says with a wry grimace and affected self-mockery, as if she were speaking to someone, "if one of those damn birds shat on me."

However, she got to her favored seat in the café without incident and in a very good mood. With a practiced eye, she peered through the greenery toward the Signorial Palace just in time to see a spill of tourists descend the steps and flow into the plaza. This was a rather larger number than usual and made up mostly of family groups, as was evident as they broke away from the mass and made their way toward the various stores and cafés. For a moment her attention was held by a little boy in an Alpine hat who ran shouting into a big flock of pigeons setting them all off into a second wild flight. When they settled down again, one, a skinny, speckled gray one, alighted on a little stone ledge about a yard and a half from where Oriane was seated. It walked back and forth importantly turning its head from side to side as it kept one or another of its bright red eyes fixed on Oriane's face. Then without more ado, it laid an egg which miraculously didn't roll off the smooth stone surface, but the pigeon could not have cared less, flew off immediately afterward.

Now a group of tourists sat down at the next table. There were four of them, Oriane was pleased to note; an older man, very hearty and robust-looking, with a red, weather-beaten face and small gray eyes, about seventy, a Westerner, Oriane decided promptly, his wife, who had all the airs and graces of a pretty woman, no longer had the looks though she appeared expensively dressed and taken care of. They were accompanied by two rather plain women in their thirties, one or both of whom might have been their daughter. After a few minutes of eavesdropping, Oriane found the girls' names were Mitzi and Bea and all three women addressed the man as Colonel; the Colonel called his wife something that sounded like "R" or "Are" and occasionally "Mother," though neither of the girls seemed to call her anything.

The four of them now looked out at the Signorial Palace and its high campanile. "This tower by that fellow in Florence, what's his name?" asked the Colonel.

"Giotto," said his wife guardedly.

"I think so," said one of the girls.

"I don't think so," said the other. Then they looked at each other with some confusion.

"I think it's just as pretty," said the wife.

"I like it better," said the girl who thought it designed by Giotto. "Simpler, you know, not so fussy."

"But if you put it next to one of our Douglas firs or

mountain hemlocks neither of them would look like much, no siree," from the Colonel.

"I like the one in Florence better," said the other girl. They must be sisters, Oriane decided. She turned away and scanned the plaza and at that moment she saw him, the ragged boy, the deaf-mute.

He was walking slowly in her direction but whether he saw her through the hedge she could not tell. His face looked pitifully thin and pinched and she wondered whether he had been sick. This time I will give him a present, Oriane decided, and she signaled to the waiter to bring her her bill. The boy was looking at the ground and once or twice she saw him stoop down to pick up cigarette butts that he carefully stowed away in an inside pocket. The waiter was mortally slow in noticing her signal, then he merely nodded and disappeared into the back of the café.

Now the boy was directly outside the hedge but with his head still turned away. "Oh, oh you . . . you, boy . . ." she started to call out, realizing at the same time that it was of no possible use. She started to wave, but still he didn't see her, but he did spy the pigeon egg on the ledge and leaped forward with astonishing speed to take possession of it.

"*Cameriere, cameriere!*" she called despairingly.

But now the boy turned and their eyes met and slowly a very sweet smile spread over his thin features. She beckoned to him eagerly using her whole hand. This time she would take him to a bakery and buy him all the bread he could eat; she would buy him shoes and a good warm sweater. Or perhaps he would prefer money. She could give him some money too.

Still smiling he beckoned back to her and began to

retreat. She beckoned to him again, he did likewise and hastened his step, and in a minute was out of sight around the corner of a building before she realized, before she remembered, that hers had been the Italian gesture of farewell.

"Well, like I say," the Colonel went on. "One of our mountain hemlocks, or a Douglas fir, let alone a giant sequoia would make all these Eyetalian towers look like nothing."

10

Dissimilar in size and shape and color to the rose leaves, the praying mantis yet achieved a kind of camouflage, masqueraded as a willow leaf or sumac blown into the thorny vine by the wind, hung down boldly inconspicuous to wait for a foolish fly to blunder within the reach of its meekly folded forelegs. The roses had finished blooming weeks earlier, and their foliage had become raggedy with summer, an ill-kept vine, the old growth had not been cut away, or the dead roses picked off, and mildew spotted the green like ash on an old man's vest. It was a hot, airless July afternoon and the sun shone through a smoky mist making the magnolia tree's pale branches look bleached and stark against the yellowing lawn. Midges and gnats droned in the shade and the rose vine on the house was as good a place as any for the praying mantis to keep his vigil.

Oriane spotted him the minute she had come out on the porch and had watched him idly for a long time, hoping that he would catch a fly while she was looking. Of course, she was talking all the while, saying that perhaps it would be cooler to sit in the house, or did they find it pleasanter to be in the open air.

Oh, yes, they all agreed, it was lovely on the porch. Jarry Holt explained that she preferred to breathe air that had been in the sun. Professor Thurby remarked mildly that he himself spent too much time indoors. His sister, Helen, said vaguely that she had always liked porches. Giles merely made little kissing noises as he sucked on his mustache and meticulously settled himself in the elaborate Hong Kong chair, wicker, with the back in the shape of an enormous light bulb—Oriane had thought it charming and unique when she had spotted it in an antique store, but now almost everybody had one. Giles liked to sit in it, however, though it was less comfortable than the other chairs, because it was so impressive and thronelike. And while Giles didn't look very regal, he did look quite nice in a clean, twinkly, granddadish sort of way. His prematurely white hair and beard together with his snow-apple complexion and bright blue eyes all had the frosted look of a dessert fresh from the refrigerator.

Oriane, sitting opposite, appeared as a mere slip of a girl or at least so she hoped with all her heart. Actually, no woman under forty-five or fifty would be likely to wear a costume that was so chic and so gaudy as that

Oriane now had on. Bare legs, dagger-heeled gold sandals, shrimp-pink nails, jangling junk jewelry completed a getup which could not be carried off unless one has a truly mature judgment backed by some twoscore years of experience.

The fact is that the morning had found Oriane extremely depressed—she had slept badly the night before; Tessa had been out with Mark until very late and while bitter memories of her own mother's watchfulness over her as a young girl had prevented Oriane's waiting up for them, this did not prevent her from remaining fretfully sleepless until long after she heard Tessa's light footsteps on the stair. Then Tessa had stayed up for some time and the minute noises that she made had found their way with almost uncanny precision across and down the hall and through two closed doors to where her mother lay rigid and purposefully unlistening.

The morning chores and cares had done little to dissipate Oriane's black mood, so once the veal galantine was garnished and placed in the refrigerator, she retired to take a long hot bath followed by a manicure and the donning of her new dress. It was really a beautiful dress, if it wasn't awful, she decided: jungle flowers rioted on a black field, orchids or Venus's-flytraps, low cut, the skirt brief as could be; it was made of cotton, albeit silky Egyptian cotton, and thus enabled Oriane to feel that it wasn't too formal for a summer day at home.

"Who's coming?" Giles asked when she finally appeared.

"The Thurbys and Jarry Holt."

"Well, you're awfully dressed up."

"You might say something nice."

"I did, I said you're awfully dressed up."

"Thank you, you're very gallant."

"Well, what should I have said?"

One could count on it, one could always and eternally count on exactly what Giles would say in any given situation. Oriane went silently into the kitchen to see to the salad. Actually, that was what she had loved so about him in the beginning. Then as she bent down to take the lettuce from the crisper she had a sudden conviction that one day soon she would simply pack her bags and go away and never come back.

A conviction that immediately evaporated leaving a little tiny residue of thought that she laughed at sardonically. Impossible.

Now Oriane reached down to the bag at the side of her chair and drew out her knitting; it lay in her lap, warm and fuzzy and light as a kitten—a sweater for Tessa —winter does come after the long hot summer and one might as well be prepared for it. The wool was a bright blue-green that would go well with the girl's flame-colored head, they had both agreed, and Tessa had picked out the pattern—the most complicated one available. Well, it's a challenge, Oriane had said with a wry smile. A challenge, she thought now, as she carefully counted the stitches, in the Year of Our Lord nineteen hundred and sixty-four, this is a challenge.

She counted twice to make sure and then shook her head, sleepy from the big meal that they had all just finished. Jarry Holt would soon be telling her that one should only serve light meals on hot days or hot meals on hot days according to some theory she'd read about in the *Reader's Digest*.

But she was mildly mistaken; Jarry began to talk

about her new "machine" for making yoghurt. "There's a place in California where the culture comes from," she said excitedly, "and you keep using it over and over."

Now the "children" came out on the porch. Oriane's mind played with the word "children" for a minute or two as she tried to contain her surprise at seeing Tessa and Mark actually settled down on the glider against the wall. To her dying day, her mother had always called her (Oriane) a child, which had bothered her especially when she was Tessa's age, but here she was doing precisely the same thing.

However, she was not prepared to have Tessa remark with all the appositeness in the world, "We thought we'd join the grownups for a while."

"Glad to have you," mumbled Giles, absently polite.

Jarry merely raised her voice slightly and continued talking. "It's not really a machine, actually a kind of hot plate, that's all there is to it, and four pyrex dishes, but it never gets very hot, uses only as much electricity as a 25-watt light bulb. I've been eating yoghurt morning, noon and night and you know it's so healthy for you. It's the Kurds or somebody in Asia who live to be a hundred and they all eat yoghurt. It does something to your intestines—I don't mean keeping you regular or things like that, but something about the parasites, or whatever they are, that is particularly important to longevity. I read about it in Aldous Huxley, I think it was, and he was writing about something in a carp's intestines that makes them live so long. Yes, carp, you know, the fish, they live hundreds of years. They don't know how long exactly because nobody ever kept track.

"And Mark, now I'm talking to you particularly."

"Yes, Mrs. Holt?"

"When you're in Europe, you be sure and go to Versailles and look in the pools there and you'll see carp there who go back to before the French Revolution. Isn't that amazing? I mean some of those carp have actually seen Marie Antoinette in person."

Mark smiled faintly. "Yes, Mrs. Holt, I'll go and visit them."

Oriane gazed up at the ceiling and caught sight of a bumbling fly and as the senses follow one another she could now hear the faintly modulated buzz it made. Then, recalling the praying mantis, she glanced down; there it was identically angled against the vine. He kept solemnly still, his forelegs folded prayerfully before a pathetically wizened little face, the pointed wings, green cutaway coat, elegant dandy legs extended below.

"But he isn't really praying, he's catching bugs," Tessa's voice literal and didactic as a schoolmarm's.

"Oh, I don't know," Mark answered. "You can't tell, maybe he is praying."

"When a bug comes along his legs will come out and get it, you'll see," Tessa insisted.

"Just the same, he might be praying now, even if he does catch a bug later on. You haven't proved a thing."

"But . . ."

Mark was grinning at her impudently. Oriane looked at his hard, shining black eyes, narrowed now into two smooth slits over high Tartar cheekbones, his lips parted in a silent laugh. He really is an extraordinarily handsome boy, she thought lazily.

"But I mean . . ." Tessa began, but Oriane's attention was switched off as if with a key—this kind of badinage went on endlessly between those two, perhaps for the benefit of their elders. Elder, older—children

130

make you older by the mere fact of their being younger. On the day you were born, Tessa, I became one whole generation older.

Those sharp saucer eyes of Jarry Holt's looked at the "children" on the glider and then at the pile of knitting on Oriane's lap, "Before you know it, Oriane, you'll be knitting for a grandchild."

"Goose run across your grave, O?" asked Giles, who when he didn't miss something felt it necessary to be jocular.

"Something like that," she answered dryly.

Of course, Jarry Holt was a good soul and did a great deal of good for a great many people, which was why one put up with hearing her talk. Now she was telling Professor Thurby and his sister the same business about yoghurt and the carp at Versailles and they appeared to be listening attentively though they had probably heard her the first time round.

In fact, Thurby managed to remark politely, "I've seen those carp at Versailles, but I never realized they were as old as that."

There were other sounds to listen to in the quiet afternoon. The click of her own knitting needles, and the minute soft rush of yarn through her fingers; the low hum of a motor in the house, cicadas in the bushes, a distant car going down the highway. Far off there was the illegal pop of an air rifle, doubtless Ted or Phil Higgins, two very resourceful boys whom no local ordinance would ever faze in the least. Their parents were proud rather than otherwise of their lawlessness, so nothing could be done.

"They're good boys, really, Mrs. Anderton. A bit on the wild side, that's all, shows they got the Higgins blood in them." Mrs. Higgins could chatter along complacently while she moistened her stamps against the brown, moldy-looking post-office sponge. That flat, honest, tolerant face traveled ponderously across her mind's landscape blanking it out as innocently and effectively as a freight train.

Now she looked at the praying mantis, wondering whether he had caught a fly after all. It was impossible to tell, of course, insects never look hungry or satisfied or old or young. Well, perhaps a specialist might discover some differences. . . .

In point of time, one might suppose, all this took place precisely midway between the building of the pyramids and the present.

"All this is ancient history," one of Giles's favorite expressions. He doesn't look like a schoolmaster for nothing and he has a way of pronouncing his words that fills you with yawns.

"All this is ancient history and I needn't go into all the details," but he invariably does. In point of time, all this took place about eight months ago. Counting back, that is, from April in Friani. How curious, though, that the present should be so diffuse in a sun-drenched Italian town, so that when you go indoors, Oriane, you blink and grope in the sudden blind, drawn darkness. Mark is a shadowy outline against a window, less shaded than the rest, profiled pile of books and papers on the table in front of him reminds you of a city sky line, a city of children's blocks. You pass through this room without disturbing him (you hope) and go into the bathroom to view your face in the mirror narrowly and critically before you get to work on it. Then although it is quite warm here and there is nothing in the glass to cause it, you see all at once that you shivered.

"Goose run across your grave, O?" from Giles. And all the particulars of this quiet afternoon come back, narrated now in that flat, emphasisless voice, going into all the details while he repeatedly says he won't because it is all ancient history.

"You will make a wonderful grandmother, knitting as well as you do." Nothing will stop good-natured, well-meaning, good-deed-doing Jarry Holt when she has an idea to worry to death. Now she turns her head and gives a broad wink at Tessa and Mark.

The poor girl blushes furiously and says with rather more warmth than she really feels, "But you haven't proved that he *is* praying."

Well, if she was going to sit there on the glider flirting with her young man, she would simply have to make the best of having everybody approve their heads off. Of course it wasn't easy, as her mother well knew, it wasn't all that easy for mothers when it comes down to it. She and Tessa had tacitly agreed not to discuss Mark other than to assure each other that he wasn't Serious, that he was Simply Passing the Time while he waited for the Fall and going to Europe and All That.

So naturally and of course it wasn't Significant that these two had been seeing each other almost every day. In fact to think of it makes Oriane shake her head and smile, he was so remarkably and innocently persistent ever since that first evening when they giddily stayed out till four in the morning.

However, Jarry, who had never stopped talking was saying that she thought Oriane ought to knit something for the charity bazaar that she was organizing. "Handmades are always in demand. You know Mrs. Thragnell who makes those little crocheted birds. We always sell every single one. They are sweet, of course. People hang them up over babies."

Now she took Helen Thurby into her conversation. "You don't knit or crochet do you, my dear?"

"I'm afraid not."

"Well, we always need volunteers with station wagons." This with a gesture toward the driveway. Helen smiled thinly. Her brother was earnestly trying to talk about world affairs with Giles, but while Giles invariably spent hours with the newspapers, he didn't seem to have much to say. Not that that makes the slightest difference to our Edward, Oriane reflected good-naturedly.

She would pack her suitcase and her trunk and simply go away and never come back. The idea that had come to her like an inspiration in the morning as she took the lettuce from the crisper.

She held the thought in her mind until it seemed to fill her whole being, globed and expanding like a marvelous iridescent bubble. Place names, postcard-picture vistas of far-off sights danced on the sliding edge of her consciousness. She drew a deep breath and abruptly returned to Jarry Holt who was saying with a weirdly inappropriate triumph in her voice, "We can always use people who will ring doorbells."

"Yes, I suppose so," Helen's blandly noncommittal answer.

Giles stood up so suddenly and determinedly that the big, unbalanced chair he'd been sitting in fell backwards against the railing. "Excuse me," he mumbled.

Without taking her eyes from the praying mantis,

Oriane saw that Mark had gotten up to right the chair. It was only polite, but at the same time there was something familial about his action that was not lost on anyone present. Meanwhile Giles shuffled into the house and slowly ascended the stairs. After a few minutes there was a broadly explanatory rushing and cascading in the pipes within and the footsteps slowly descended the stairs with undeniable majesty, but when they reached the hall, instead of coming toward the porch, they turned aside, penetrated the dining room, then changed their sound as they reached the kitchen tiles. There was the faint click of the refrigerator door being opened— Giles had had two helpings of the blancmange at dinner, but though yearning for a third had not wanted to take it in front of the company; he would return presently with a little guilty line of white on his mustache.

"Can't I offer you something cold to drink?" Oriane said full of conscience. And, after everyone's reassuring no-no's, added that she was going to get herself something.

"Well, some ice water," Helen Thurby allowed.

Now they all wanted glasses of ice water except for Jarry who preferred her water without ice, merely cold from the tap and Tessa and Mark rose simultaneously to fetch some. Well, Tessa could be trusted to get her father to use a napkin before he returned to the company.

In the slight silence that followed the young people's going indoors, Jarry's voice sounded unusually loud and flat. "I must say, Oriane, I seem to hear the sound of wedding bells in the not-too-distant future."

"Really?" Keep it calm and casual, keep on knitting, it shouldn't bother you in the least in any case. Knit two, purl two, you've been thinking the same thing yourself, ribbing on the collar, the praying mantis has never moved yet, remarkable how he can keep so still, has all the time in the world, of course.

"I think you know more than you're telling," Jarry persisted.

"I always know more than I tell," Oriane returned airily.

"It's to be hoped that a lady will never tell as much as she knows," the good professor remarked kindly. He was trying to rescue her, Oriane knew, and thanked him in her heart for the effort, though she knew Jarry would never be diverted.

"Seriously, Oriane, you must be very happy about it, you've always been so fond of Mark."

Oriane stared out over the lawn, seriously she must be very happy about it, seriously, she would pack some bags, never mind the trunk, just suitcases, and simply go away; a strange dry anguish made her throat contract painfully, will they never get here with the water? Seriously, she must be very happy, delighted, gratified—so many words to describe a state of being that simply did not exist for her, though in all the next few weeks and months of her life they would be ever on her lips or flowing from her pen.

Lint from the wool on her lap had accumulated on her hands and up the insides of her bare arms; odd that the soft, harmless, almost invisible stuff seemed to be attacking her skin like a cloud of stinging gnats.

"It's nothing very serious. After all, he's going away so soon and they're both so young."

"Nonsense, they're quite old enough. Parents simply never realize it when their children grow up."

"There's also the problem of what would they live on. He only gets a pittance besides his transportation. And Giles certainly can't support them, and Mr. Norwood's stroke . . ." There was a kind of relief which she thought came from speaking so practically.

Tessa came first, carrying the big pitcher of water in one hand and holding the door open for Mark with the other. He carried the tray of glasses filled with ice, but he had taken one of her smallest trays, Oriane noticed, so that it took tremendous concentration and steadiness to keep the glasses in place; an effort that was made even more difficult in that they were both laughing.

Neither of them had ever looked more handsome, Oriane realized, and she found the words forming calmly in her mind, Jarry, of course, is perfectly right, they are in love with each other. She caught sight of Giles looming behind them in the dark hall, his large, pale head rising like a full moon over Mark's left shoulder.

Now everyone was taking a glass and Tessa was filling them from her pitcher. Oriane realized that the hand she had reached out for her water was trembling and she raised the glass immediately to her lips in an attempt to hide her agitation, this only served, however, to make her spill some of the water down the front of her dress. What could be more natural than that they should love each other?

Jarry was condemning ice water, which she said chilled the membrane that lined the walls of the stomach. Then, as if in confirmation, Oriane felt a hard, sharp pain in her own stomach, a sensation of having swallowed a piece of jagged ice. Jarry would probably say that she was not losing a daughter, that she was gaining a son. She had always wanted a son. She had always wanted Mark for a son. But the joke of it was that she was really losing them both.

Even as she was losing them both at this instant. Instead of sitting down after serving the water the children were excusing themselves. They had to go now, they said; they held hands lightly and smilingly said good-bye and everybody smiled at them and all the transparent reasons they gave for leaving so soon.

Oriane watched them go down the lawn toward the Hollow. The grass was yellowed and tired-looking from the drought, but the trees in the Hollow above the little stream were fresh and green; the couple walked demurely over the grass, then suddenly, like the frisky young creatures they were, they began to run, while they who sat on the porch like bumps on a log watched and laughed good-naturedly.

"Now seriously," Jarry began insufferably. However, quite soon I shall be far away. France, Spain, Italy. The Eiffel Tower, Escorial, the Colosseum. The pain in her stomach had vanished as quickly as it had come; her fingers were knitting now with marvelous, unthinking mechanical precision.

She raised her eyes once more to the lawn; the children were just at that moment disappearing under the trees, but Tessa turned and waved. The effect on Oriane was extraordinary and instantaneous. Her consciousness seemed to leap across that wide space and for a dizzying interval it appeared to her that it was she, herself, Oriane, who walked on that damp, soft ground beside her beloved, that it was she now taking one backward glance at the little group on the porch, immobilized like flies in amber to stay for all eternity, but as she raised her hand to wave, the illusion broke and it was the mother on the porch waving at the two lovers below by the stream.

Oriane sighed and looked at the praying mantis; it was still there though it had moved a little higher on the vine. Also, it did look as though it were praying. Double camouflage, as leaf to bug, as suppliant to human eyes.

"Oriane, darling, you haven't heard a word I've been saying. But you can't fool me."

Oriane looked steadily into those friendly, blue, saucer eyes and, without parting her lips, she smiled as sweetly as she knew how.

11

I saw very little of Oriane that last summer she was in Princeton. We were away till mid-August in Milwaukee, where Steve taught in the University of Wisconsin summer program. Thus, most of what I know of Oriane at that time is secondhand, based on letters from her friends, though Oriane did write me a couple of her typically harebrained and frantic notes. Also, of course, there's all the talk that has gone on afterward, and all the conjectures and all the theories, whatever they might be worth.

However, the "facts" themselves are strictly small order and routine—by the third week in July, Tessa and

Mark had decided to marry, and for the rest of the time up to the day of the wedding, set on the Saturday before Labor Day, Oriane was apparently completely occupied with helping her daughter shop for her trousseau, plan for her trip to Europe, for of course Mark's project to study in Germany on his Fulbright was unchanged, and finally with the wedding preparations which tended to overshadow everything else.

As far as anyone is able to judge, there was nothing out of the ordinary here, though, of course, Oriane, being Oriane, tended to overreact to every business and dramatize every trifling inconvenience or delay as it arose.

For instance, there was something that went wrong in the printing of the wedding announcements which entailed not only terrible scenes with the printer, but blow-by-blow descriptions of them; then there was a quarrel with her daughter—Tessa and Mark, it appeared, had wanted a small and quiet ceremony with only their parents and a few close friends attending.

All the particulars of this "difference of opinion" were broadcast far and wide—I even heard about it in Milwaukee, and while I thought that Tessa showed rare good sense, I didn't think she'd ever get her way. I was right, of course, and according to Oriane, Tessa's reluctance to "see reason" stemmed from her reaction to her typhoid and smallpox inoculations. Oriane wrote me of this, adding the astonishing last line which might have warned me, but of course it didn't. "Tessa hasn't been herself since she had those shots. I don't know why, I had them myself for the hell of it and there was nothing to it, sore arm for a week and the slightest swelling in the world."

In any case, Tessa seems to have been pretty much snowed under and Oriane carried everything before her. And the rest of us were fairly blinded by all that energy, merely saying among ourselves that Oriane was "too good a mother" or "too enthusiastic," that she was "doing too much for them," that she was "too generous." Presently the word got round that since lack of money had been the main obstacle to an early wedding, Oriane had come across "too handsomely," settling $10,000 on her daughter from a legacy of her mother's which no one had known about till now.

In smaller ways too, I'm told, Oriane outdid herself, leaving nothing to chance; in effect, leaving nothing to her daughter's initiative. From shopping for a far more elaborate trousseau than Tessa had ever thought of, to taking over the young people's social life. She sent them far and wide to call on distant relatives, explaining ingenuously, "They will send checks anyway, but if they get their money's worth, get a chance to get acquainted with the children and give them advice, their checks will be bigger." Then several times a week Oriane gave little dinners or after-dinner got-togethers, inviting this person and that person who had been to Europe or who was going there, getting introductions and information. "Tessa simply has no idea what life will be like over there. I'm not worried about Mark, he has his work, but Tessa can't just sit around doing nothing," Oriane would say with a worldly simper.

As if all this were not enough, in one burst of energy, Oriane visited some fourteen travel agencies and government tourist bureaus to pick up brochures; previously she had been to the library a number of times bringing home armloads of books—whether or not Tessa had time to look at any of this is open to question, but Oriane, it appears, pored over them, memorizing whole portions, in order, she said, to pass on pointers to the children.

Of course, in the clear, fine light of hindsight, it's easy enough to see what Oriane was really up to, but it must be admitted that a better camouflage could hardly be imagined. No one is really interested in the weddings of one's friends' children, other than to benignly wish them well, so Oriane's constant talk and constant busyness served marvelously to divert our attention by boring us to extinction.

But so it went. Then one day after I got back from Milwaukee, Oriane called up to ask me if the water in Italy is safe to drink. I just said patiently, yes it is, but I had understood that Mark and Tessa were going to Germany.

"Well, all of Europe will be their province, really," Oriane said so grandly that I never gave the matter another thought.

However, that phone call did produce an invitation to Spook Hollow. She means to pick my brains about Italy, I supposed a bit acidly, but I liked Oriane anyway and I said I'd go.

*

Thus one fine August day I went out to Oriane's for lunch. As I drove up to the house, she waved to me gaily from a sunny spot on the lawn that was half hidden from the driveway by a thin screen of lilac bushes. I parked the car in the turnaround back of the house and took my time about getting out because I couldn't decide whether to go into the house or to join

Oriane on the lawn. After a few minutes' hesitation, I started for the house.

The door was wide open, but there was not a soul anywhere. Actually I had known that Giles would be working and I assumed that Tessa was off somewhere, but I wasn't sure that I was the only guest. The table set for two on the terrace assured me on this point, so there was really nothing to do except to go back outside. Which eventually I did, though I gained a little more time going to the bathroom and combing my hair.

What made me so shy was the fact that Oriane was stark naked.

Well, I told myself, after all there's nothing so much in one woman seeing another in the nude, and if she didn't care, why should I? I walked across the sunny lawn. The weather was incredibly beautiful, an out-of-season autumn day; the sun was hot, and the air a little cold, directly ahead of me was a small maple tree, one branch of which had turned a lovely buttery yellow, beyond it the lawn slanted in a steep grade down to the little brook that glistened through a feathery haze of trembling birch leaves. A bird flew over my head.

"Well, you certainly did take your time!"

"Sorry, I had to go to the john." I still felt very much embarrassed, she seemed so very large and at the same time vulnerable in her nakedness; I didn't want to look at her and I didn't want not to look at her. Well, at least for a while I could be very busy lighting a cigarette. Oriane threw me a pillow which I sat down on. She had been lying on her stomach, now she flipped herself over so that heap of wheat set about with lilies, so to speak, offered itself innocently to the sun's gaze and mine.

"What if anyone came?" I asked finally.

"So what? They'd see a sight."

My cigarette had gone out so I had to relight it.

"Look," she said suddenly, "one's body is nothing to be ashamed of and don't you waste your youth being ashamed of yours."

"I don't think I am," I said weakly.

"Voice of experience speaking. In two years' time I won't be fit to be seen by candlelight. See my breasts like two gunny sacks?" (Nothing could have been less true.) "Once upon a time they were round and firm like yours. The skin on my elbows is getting loose and turning into sandpaper and my neck is going. When I put my arms over my head I have two hideous dimples right in the middle of each shoulder as big as navels. You can learn lots about yourself if you spread it out quietly in the light of day and the pity of it is all the time I was young and decent I threw it away by not even knowing I had it.

"I learned the hard way, of course. That's the way I always learn things. Six months in the hospital with nothing to do but contemplate the universe and the marvelous equipment we're each endowed with."

Oriane sat up now and plucked nervously at the leaves of grass in front of her. "I'm talking about the automobile accident. I mean afterwards, of course." She raised her chin and seemed to be talking to the sky. "Giles was driving and never had a scratch on him . . . one of those things." The glare, I suppose, made her narrow her eyes, but it gave her a shrewd, rather calculating look which was vaguely unpleasant. What she said next was spoken very quickly and was very hard to follow. Something like, "Three kids died in that accident. College students. I had that to think about too and

Giles would come in and say, 'It's fate, their number was up, so to speak.' I was out of my head some of the time and then he'd come in and say that to me."

She lay down again, restlessly crossing her arms under her head. "You know that first time I met you, you had seen me playing tennis and you made some remark about it. Do you remember that? And how I told you a long story about being a finalist in Forest Hills in 1946. I don't know what got into me, only I suppose I thought I'd never see you again. I wanted to shoot myself afterwards.

"Well the fact is that summer in 1946 was when I was in the hospital. One of the attendants was a tennis buff and he had the radio turned on for every loving match in Forest Hills. He was a nice young fellow, not so good-looking but he had a wonderful smile. Of course he was busy a lot of the time, so I kept track of all the scores and who was playing and all that.

"It was really very good therapy, gave me something to think about besides all those broken bones and those poor kids. So clean, so to speak, and *real*. I don't know what all."

She paused for a long moment and then sighed. "Well, now I've got that off my chest and the moral of this story is don't despise what God gave you till it's too late to do anything else. Now I think it's time for us to go in and have lunch. I'm hungry enough to eat dog."

She put on a terry-cloth robe and a pair of scuffs, picked up the blanket and the pillows. "Come on, I'll race you to the house."

Mark was there in the hall when we got in. Barely giving him time to greet us, Oriane asked him with a fiend's smile, "By the way, did you ever return my binoculars?"

146

The boy seemed genuinely confused. "Binoculars?"

"I loaned you my pair ages ago."

"Well, I'll have to take a look."

The weight of the blankets and pillows she held in one arm had pulled the robe awry on that side leaving a great gap in front. She could have righted it with her free hand but she did nothing of the sort. Merely gestured vaguely and said, "Look diligently."

"What time is Tess coming back?"

"Oh, Tess. Three, three-thirty, I think." She began to cough. "That damn cold." She coughed and coughed. Mark pounded her on the back which did no good at all, then, when he went to fetch her a glass of water, the coughing subsided and, without waiting for him to return, she went off upstairs to dress.

I don't know if he did come back with the water. I went out on the terrace and smoked a cigarette. I had just remembered that Giles never had learned to drive a car because of his poor eyesight.

12

It rained on Tessa's wedding day. A cold, raw rain lashed by a northeast wind, with all the portents indicating that there would be no clearing before evening, if then. This, of course, worked hob with Oriane's plans to have the reception on the lawn where people would have a chance to move around. Well, there were stand-by plans if they had to be in the house. Oriane got up at dawn to rearrange the furniture.

Not dawn precisely, it was merely light enough to move about the house without bumping into things. And Oriane went softly around, peering into dark mirrors that gave back only the merest shadow of a reflection; automatically she picked up her brush from the dressing table, then almost at once decided to leave dressing her hair till later; she turned to look at Giles asleep, hugely humped on the bed, sleep well, she said bitterly, passed on down the hall and peeked in Tessa's room. She sleeps, Oriane thought with amazement. The girl had always slept as if arranged on the bed, on her back with her hands clasped loosely over her breast, her hair spread out on the pillow like a sunburst pricked out under her head. Oriane stood for a long while at the door listening to the rapt somnolent breathing. She sleeps.

Oh my God, she is asleep. Oriane realized that she was weeping. Easy tears that left a little cool track on her cheeks and dropped on her clenched hand. Oriane moved over to the window, but it was impossible to tell whether it was raining. It wasn't raining hard, whatever it was, but the strange light-dark sky held no stars, so perhaps it was raining. Oriane studied the stretch of lawn till it disappeared into a miasma of shadow. But children do sleep, she thought tenderly.

Now she went to the closet to look at Tessa's wedding dress. It occupied the space like a queen, silky and soft and glimmering palely; all the other clothes were pushed respectfully away from it—the clothes that were left, that is, dresses that Tessa was leaving behind and the one or two things she had left out till the last minute, the rest had all been long since packed in suitcases and the trunk.

After a moment, Oriane took the dress out and, standing before the cool, dark, full-length mirror, held it up to herself. She could make out the drifting whiteness with her dark head above. Very gravely and slowly she bowed to the image. Then suddenly she became aware that Tessa's breathing had altered, it was regular still but shallower. Oriane turned around quickly and for a moment she thought the girl's eyes were open, but no, when Oriane bent closer, she could see that they were closed. However, she returned the dress to the closet and tiptoed quickly from the room.

Down in the kitchen, she heated up some coffee and listened to the weather report on the radio. No, there was no reprieve, rain was already falling in the metropolitan area, temperatures were in the chilly fifties, barometric pressure 30.2 and steady, winds in the northeast at ten to twenty miles an hour.

That, of course, was that. After she finished her coffee, Oriane smoked a cigarette and made out a few lists. She must have made hundreds of lists in the past two months, she thought wryly and looked at her handwriting with sleep-famished eyes. The lists were stuck up all over the place and presently Giles would find them and take them down. Oriane smiled briefly if a bit grimly.

The heavy furniture in the living room would have to wait till later, but working slowly and ploddingly, barefooted as a peasant, Oriane removed all the small tables and chairs to the study. It meant that people would have to stand up, but they simply wouldn't be able to get in otherwise. Perhaps stand-up affairs are more fun anyway, one doesn't get stuck with people you don't like, you can simply walk off.

It was growing lighter outside, but gloomy and overcast, a faint grayish streak in the east was all the sun she would see that day, in a sky hung with layer upon layer of dimpled clouds. The trees against the house moved restlessly like animals trying to shake off the wet. Oh the trees, thought Oriane with a kind of queer relief that exasperation gives. They grew much too close to the house and in summer hogged all the light.

And now the memory came of all the endless discussions of how to brighten up the living room. In fact, it seemed as if she and Giles had rarely talked of anything else, rather this single conversation, as it were, seemed to thread itself pointlessly through the years, or perhaps, instead of being pointless, it was the code and cipher by which they managed to maintain contact with each other. So now she could hear her voice saying, "Really, Giles, we must start thinking about taking down some of the trees."

"Yes," Giles would return judiciously, "the trees are getting pretty big." He would stroke his beard thoughtfully, and like the unvarying magic attributes in a fairy tale would come the toting up of the special virtues of each tree that was its charm and patent for survival.

The maple tree was so tall and spectacularly beautiful in the fall, next was the elm, somewhat sickly, but the only elm in the vicinity to have survived Dutch elm disease. The cedar tree was one of the oldest and thickest in the county, it all but strangled a delicately beautiful, self-planted dogwood. Next was the cherry tree, which had reached a stupendous size, with the spreading branches of a field-grown oak; it still bore a huge harvest of magnificent oxeye cherries. So it went for the silver fir, the flowering cherry, the ginkgo, the star magnolia. Oriane went upstairs to dress with the names of the trees still echoing in her ears.

Now the reception was going full tilt. Mark was standing next to the window with Ida Dingman and Edna

Trotter, Tessa was next to the door with a shy young cousin named George Hathaway, who had acted as an usher; he was a tall, extremely thin youth who looked mortified in his not-quite-fitting striped pants and cutaway. Jarry Holt had just stridden up, holding in one hand what looked to be a two-quart jar of wheat germ and a small bottle of chlorine tablets.

"I'm sorry, dear," she said in a businesslike way, "I meant to give you these before. My sister had the pills left over from her trip to Mexico. I asked the druggist about them and he said they don't deteriorate, so you take them along. Now, this is wheat germ, sprinkle it on your strudel. The Europeans don't know anything about vitamins. That's why they're all so small and have all those wars."

Jarry narrowed her eyes into little thin crescents of blue. "I must say, child, you're a quick worker, but none of us are very surprised. Good luck and you look very happy." Her dry lips pecked at the girl's cheek, then in her best no-nonsense voice she remarked, "Look, I know you probably shan't want to start an infant right away, but when the time comes just remember that a douche of two quarts of water with two tablespoons of bicarbonate of soda can work wonders."

The young George Hathaway blushed furiously, but fortunately at this point Patricia Crory sidled up to tell them, "It was a lovely, lovely wedding. And so romantic. I think weddings are always romantic though."

"But I'm not losing a son," Mrs. Norwood shouted at the top of her lungs, "I'm gaining a daughter." She was dressed in a cloud of sunset-pink voile, rainbow streamers from a big hat hung girlishly down her broad back, a dewy wetness sat on her lips and eyes and from time to time she would put her hands together over her bosom and make her proclamation and at the same time look around Oriane's living room with a proprietary air. Mr. Norwood was dressed in a tuxedo that was so old that it was turning purple, it had pointed satin lapels and the white carnation Mrs. Norwood had put in his buttonhole kept falling out, because she had cut the stem too short. He sat in a chair in the corner of the room and weakness made him sweat. He told everybody who would listen about the circumstances of his two strokes and he appeared very much at a loss as to why he was there. He kept looking at the blue veins in his wrist where the treacherous blood ran through so furiously that it threatened his life with every breath he took.

"The spoons are lovely, Patricia," Tessa said with some effort.

"Yes. Pappa brought them from Salzburg in '98. They're souvenir spoons really, but Sister says they're coming back."

Oriane strolled through her company; she was wearing a beautiful gold-colored dress from Bergdorf's, a strange, cream-and-purple orchid on her shoulder; her face was so made-up and lacquered over that no one would guess that sleeplessness was the chief ingredient of that queer wooden look. She paused for a moment beside Patricia Crory and, having caught the word Salzburg, murmured like a sleepwalker, "Mozart."

"Yes," Patricia said eagerly. "Of course, Mozart." She wriggled her shoulders. "Mozart was born in Salzburg on January 27th, 1756, and I was born on his birthday exactly one hundred and fifty years later. Oh, Oriane dear, I wanted to tell you how lovely it's all been and how marvelous to have a wedding on the Labor Day

153

weekend when one is always feeling so let down to have summer over with. And you know, we've never done anything on the Labor Day weekend because Sister's afraid of the traffic, but now I've had something to look forward to all last month."

"Thank you, Patricia."

Oriane looked at the gold clock on the mantel that said a quarter past four and tried to remember whether she had set it properly that morning. It was an ancient timepiece that she had found in a little store in Freehold, but it lost half an hour in the week; she remembered thinking that morning that she ought to set it forward, but she couldn't remember whether she had done so in all the confusion. Surely though, today is the longest day of my life, she thought, as she looked back over the long corridors of seconds and minutes and hours that separated her from the morning, and mirror image, so to speak, equally endless, that she must still traverse before she slept.

Meanwhile, little Mrs. Weir had come over to her and was whispering in her ear that she thought Tessa "made" a beautiful bride.

"Thank you, Lotte."

"And her dress is so lovely."

Tired as she was, Oriane didn't miss it when Tessa's eyes flickered over her face, which made her wonder guiltily for the twentieth time that day whether Tessa had been asleep when she had held the dress up in front of the mirror. Tessa had said nothing, only these tiny looks now and again seemed to give her away.

"We just love the salad bowl, Mrs. Weir," Tessa said dutifully.

Smiling abstractedly, Oriane drifted away with some

idea of rescuing Mark from Ida Dingman and Edna Trotter who doubtless were discussing illnesses of one sort or another. Actually the poor old things were as twittery as two girls while Mark explained to them in a patient voice that showed he'd already explained this to almost everyone there, "No, our ship doesn't sail till tomorrow and we're spending the night in New York. At the Plaza."

"At the Plaza!" Ida exclaimed with a little squeal.

"Not at the Princeton Inn!"

This, apparently, was a great joke because both the women roared with laughter while Oriane and Mark looked on with faint smiles quite unable to see any humor in the remark.

Edna Trotter was the first to recover and she did so with a little sigh and the statement that she'd only stayed in a New York hotel once, at the Windsor, and that was on the occasion of her poor niece's funeral.

This naturally sobered Ida Dingman, and Edna went on to explain that the niece was really Mr. Trotter's niece and she had only met her a few times. There followed the long and intricate story of the unhappy niece who had been ill for years but didn't die of what she was sick with, Mrs. Trotter didn't think, she was under the impression that there were "complications."

Oriane stopped listening quite soon and when Edna paused for breath, she slipped her arm through Mark's and said she had to borrow him for a minute, and she led him away.

Across the entire length of the room, then into the hall, but there were still more guests here and she continued with him out to the porch where despite the cold and the damp she was glad to stop for a moment.

She touched him lightly on the shoulder. "Do you have a cigarette?" she asked him tenderly.

"Why yes, Oriane, sure." With greedy eyes she watched his long, hard hands searching his pockets, then looked at the way his fingers curled loosely around the pack of cigarettes and the matches. As he lighted it for her, she puffed too hard as usual, making so much smoke that it got in her eyes causing them to sting and tear. She turned away to hide the weepiness, which though it derived from the mechanical irritation of the smoke seemed to her to betoken so much else besides.

She tried to speak gaily, but her voice was muffled and rather hoarse. "I thought it was time to rescue you."

"Gee, Oriane, thanks."

"And Mark, I need rescuing too." Her great, shining eyes turned to him with such intensity and passion that the light bantering answer he had in reply seemed particularly dismal and inadequate.

"Gosh sure, Oriane, any time. The white horse and the strong right arm are always at your service." He ducked his head in embarrassment and added gently, "You know, Tess and I will both be very homesick for you."

Her face hardened slightly. "Yes, that is most kind of you to say."

He waited guardedly for her to continue, but when she did not, he shrugged apologetically and staring at the uneven, spotty matting on the floor said slowly, "You know, Oriane, I'm not as sharp as sometimes. It's . . . it's been quite a day. I mean I'm sorry, I don't understand."

His confusion and embarrassment were compounded when Oriane suddenly broke into peals of laughter.

Then she put up her hand and pulling his head down by the forelock stared into his eyes.

"I'm not bad-looking, am I, Mark?"

"No," was all he managed.

"And you've always liked me?"

"Yes."

"And I love you, Mark. I know you'll understand and I know you'll help me." Then she went on to explain what she wanted with such a rush of words that he was lucky if he caught one out of three, punctuating every sentence with "you see?," "you see?," "you see, don't you, oh Mark, you do see!"

❋

Cold, deathly pale, with the damp from the outside still clinging glistening in her hair, Oriane moved silently among her guests. No one who saw her then would ever forget that appearance, yet at the time no one seemed to remark it, no one turned his head, the conversations went on in the safe, conventional grooves, "a lovely bride . . . a pity, the weather . . . so romantic . . . traveling, sailing on the *Bremen* in the morning, yes, going straight to Germany . . ."

Presently, Oriane drifted into the dining room where she came on Professor Thurby talking to the Greenes; at their elbows but not quite talking to them was a familiar-looking fat man whom she couldn't place—some friend of the Norwoods' perhaps, but before she had a chance to open her mouth the fat man handed her a glass of champagne.

Smiling perfunctorily at him and at the Greenes to whom she had already spoken at some length, she held out her left hand to the Professor and said archly, "Oh

Ed, I've been looking all over for you. I was afraid you had decided to stay in Maine for another month." Out of the corner of her eye she saw the fat man open his mouth to speak so she hurried on, "And I know you love Septembers there more than anything in the world."

"May I emend that to 'many things' to make it entirely express my feelings." Thurby smiled timidly and turning to Sigrid remarked, "It isn't often I have occasion to correct Oriane." The speech was too much for him and made him blush furiously and, alas, his embarrassment was contagious; the little silence that followed gave the fat man his chance to break into the conversation.

"Well," he said, "let's everybody drink up, to the newlyweds, God bless 'em." He smiled moistly and held out his glass to click against the others.

All the familiar furniture of the room had been replaced by the caterer's long tables except for the sideboard and the mirror above it. Oriane, turning and raising the glass, suddenly caught sight of her own image surprised in the act of forcing herself to smile at the fat man who was now muttering something about "fizzy water."

"I beg your pardon," Oriane said absently, her eyes still fixed on the mirror.

"The ladies always go for champagne, I notice."

"Yes." The woman in the mirror looked like a stranger; Oriane could examine her impersonally, noticing that haggard, bitter expression with some surprise. A smile made it worse, she thought dispassionately, as the turned-up mouth emphasized the long, hard lines that scored her cheeks. She pressed the rim of her glass against her lip and half closed her eyes pretending to concentrate on the flavor of the wine and watched the effect in the mirror. Abruptly the mirror seemed to change and darken and she saw herself with the white wedding dress held up before her as she bowed gravely to herself.

"Look, do you want to sit down or anything?" She heard the fat man speaking to her from a great distance away and for a moment she looked blankly from him to Thurby and back again, unable to grasp who had spoken to her.

"Yes, do sit down, Oriane," said Thurby.

"What? Oh, no thank you." She looked at the fat man now and recalled that only a few seconds before she had been talking to him, something about women liking champagne. The Greenes had been there too, but now they had retired to the other end of the table.

"You looked funny for a minute," the fat man said persistently.

"Oh?"

"I think you really should sit down, Oriane," Thurby said anxiously.

"Oh, no thank you."

She smiled formally. She did feel queer and dizzy and she did want to sit down. But that would never do. Probably if she ate something she would feel better. She looked over at the table. But no, she didn't want to eat.

"Well, you look better now, anyway," said the fat man kindly. She realized that he was a kind, good man in spite of his grotesque appearance. Again she tried to place him, could he be one of the men in Giles's car pool? Not that it mattered, in fact some of his virtue derived from his anonymity. Just the same she wished he would go away; but he was speaking again, fussily and bunglingly and the effort attested to his good nature.

"My wife told me I was to be sure and *not* congratulate the bride, I'm only supposed to congratulate the groom." Then in case she mistook him, he added hastily, "Not that I don't think the world of young Mark, but you're never supposed to congratulate a bride because getting a husband isn't getting a prize package no matter who he is, but a good woman is. I mean that's how my wife explained it. Says it's politeness anyhow." He laughed suddenly, showing a good many gold-capped teeth.

Abruptly the man turned serious, "Weddings take you back."

"Yes?"

"Weddings and funerals both. Even christenings. They all take you back and make you think. Well, here's cheers." He lifted his glass and moved diffidently away.

Professor Thurby cleared his throat, but all he managed to say was, "Well . . ."

"Oh Ed," she said feelingly, "I'm really glad you're here."

He pressed her hand. "I am glad too, Oriane, sincerely glad."

Now Giles came in. Twined around him like two climbing roses, one on either side, dressed in pink silk, albeit dusty pink, the Dorothy Perkins theme predominated, these two who were Tessa's college friends, the bridesmaids, Marcia Temple and Betty Bones. The former was a tall, serious-appearing girl, the latter a vivacious but severe blonde who bragged that her name had launched a thousand jokes.

"Hello there," one of them said expansively, though patronizingly.

The girls sinuously and girlishly disengaged themselves from Giles the better to devote themselves to the food. Betty cast a predatory glance over the laden table and pounced on a smoked-salmon-and-cream-cheese canapé, snapped it up. "Lots and lots of goodies," she commented in a businesslike way.

"A most perspicacious girl we have here," said Marcia.

"Yes dahling," from Betty who now gobbled down caviar on a toast round followed by some cheese puffs.

"God, you're a pig."

"Shrewdly put, my deah, shrewdly put. But how about digging in yourself. Let that thin gut of yours catch up with the fat head." Betty set the example with a deviled egg, a sausage-in-a-jacket and some olives stuffed with almonds.

All the while Giles was snorting with laughter at such high spirits. Randy old goat, was Oriane's immediate reaction, thus forgiving herself in advance for any unhappiness she might cause him.

Meanwhile Professor Thurby had said thoughtfully, "So they embark for Cythera tomorrow."

Preoccupied, Oriane replied automatically, "No, they're going direct to Germany." But she caught her mistake almost at once and laughed.

"You're worn out, my dear. I have a little plan. To take you back to Deer Island with me, which I greatly recommend in September as I believe you know."

He really meant it and Oriane was touched. "I'd love

to go. Indeed I would. I promise that one September I will come."

"Ah yes, as Swift tells us, promises and piecrust are made to be broken."

"Oh, good heavens, the cake! You must excuse me, Ed darling, I have to tell them to bring in the cake."

Smiling and patting his arm, she hurried toward the kitchen, giving a wide berth to Giles and the girls, however, but noticing as she passed that he had his mouth open and was letting Betty fill it with an asparagus tip wrapped in ham. At the door Oriane turned around and threw a kiss to the good professor, who was still watching her.

❋

Oriane was waiting for Tessa when Marcia Temple and Betty Bones brought her up to her room to change. Tessa was white and drawn, and her smile when she saw her mother was nervous and unfriendly while she let the girls push her into the chair and even smoked the cigarette that the frantic Betty Bones had thrust into her hand. "Dahling, have a weed and recover." Meanwhile Marcia had opened a window and great, damp wafts of air blew into the room.

"But it's freezing in here," Tessa complained.

"A bad sign," said Betty.

"A very bad sign." Marcia glanced at Oriane and winked.

"Brides . . ." said Betty darkly and coughed affectedly behind her hand.

"Brides, of course." Marcia winked again.

Oriane laughed uneasily, the raw air was like an ice compress laid on her skin.

162

"Seriously, Tessa dahling, we want to tell you something."

"Yes, seriously, as Betty says, it's serious."

"Yes, out of every two, one is the more serious. Marcia is the serious one."

"But that's not to say that Betty isn't very serious too."

"We're both very serious."

"Seriously, dahling, we want to tell you the significance of throwing rice at weddings."

Then with whoops of wild laughter, the two maniacs pulled Tessa's dress off her and helped her into her little blue traveling suit. "Now fix your face," they said and pushed her into the bathroom. "We'll meet you downstairs. We have a feeling that mother and daughter want to talk and four's a crowd. Oh, and don't forget to put on your shoes. It would never do to let your husband know he's married a beatnik."

The moment she was alone, Oriane in one sweeping motion removed her gold-colored dress and kicked off her golden sandals. Then from a hook inside the closet, she took out a two-piece gray woolen dress and slipped it on. The closet also yielded a pair of gray suède pumps. In addition it contained her vanity case, an overnight bag, a large, brand-new Samsonite pullman, and an old brown suitcase with a torn, peeling sticker that advertised the President Taft Hotel. These Oriane lined up against the wall by the door. Next she removed from the closet her tweed coat, a black hat, and an umbrella, which she placed on top of the suitcases; she returned to the closet for a traveling garment bag into which she stowed the golden dress. She dropped the sandals into two side pockets, and folding the bag in half, zippered it all around. Then taking it by the handle, she placed it on the floor with her other suitcases. Last of all, she took from the closet an outsized handbag with shoulder straps and zippered pockets.

All this was the work of a few seconds, and before Tessa returned from the bathroom, Oriane had time to touch up her make-up and smooth her hair; she even had time to pick up Tessa's wedding dress which the girls had merely laid across the foot of the bed. She had put it on its special hanger and was carefully putting it away when she heard Tessa's voice. "Mother . . . tell me what's going on?"

"Why it's very simple, my dear, I'm going away."

"Mark said . . ."

"Yes, I've arranged everything with Mark. You see, in a few minutes one of the waiters will take my things down and put them in the trunk of the car. Then after you and Mark leave, you will wait for me down by the road." Oriane moved over to the window and ducking her head sideways stared out at the darkening trees; she raised her hand to her face in that habitual gesture of hers.

"Then you'll drive me out to the airport," she added almost as an afterthought. Now she twisted the pull cord on the shade into a kind of cat's cradle on one hand, weaving it back and forth between her fingers. At length she pulled her hand away and straightened the cord.

"But . . . I don't understand . . . where are you going, why . . ."

"We'll talk about that later. We can talk about it on the way. I mean I know it's a lot to ask you . . . at this point, that is . . . it will mean so much to me, it will help me so. I mean I can remember your being there with me. I . . . Oh Tessa, forgive me. Tessa . . . I want to . . . help you put on your shoes."

164

Then before the startled girl knew what was happening, Oriane knelt down and slipped one and then the other shoe on her feet.

"Mother, oh Mother."

Oriane leaned backwards and raised her chin to laugh that loud, crowing, remarkable laugh that she had, that for all its hoarseness was very attractive as it expressed such open mirth and amusement. "Oh my darling, shoes bring good luck. Now help me up."

She took Tessa's hand, but with the lightness of air sprang to her feet, "Now we are ready," she said.

13

The young Italian spoke to Oriane merely to ask the way. He had to repeat the question twice because even after six months she spoke so little of the language. Finally he pointed and said, "Via Roma?"

"*Sì.*" Oriane motioned helplessly. The street was two blocks up and across the market square to the left. "*A destra.*"

"*A sinistra, signora?*"

Yes, of course, sinister. On the left hand. She was left-handed too. Maladroit. The bony hand covered the lower part of her face. It should have shaded her eyes against the sinking sun that shone in her face blinding her. She could hardly see the young man, boy almost, except that his hair was rather long and curly and he was unusually tall and slender. He walked slowly through the red sunshine to the right, past the terrace where she stood. She turned her head and watched him because there was something in the way he moved that caught her attention, graceful and lithe as a young animal, but he limped slightly, almost too little to be noticed, favoring one foot casually, one who is hurt but ignores the pain, one perhaps who does not truly feel the pain. He disappeared behind the wall of the cathedral. To the right.

She frowned. *A destra, a sinistra,* how stupid to forget always. *Destra* sounded more left to her than *sinistra,* dextrous, skillful, right. Surely since he had corrected her he had understood her, the road was to the left. She stared at the bricks in the wall where the stucco had molded away; they were longer and flatter than the bricks at home, brown as the brown bare earth in the vineyards, a brown that was gray and beige, not red, except that the setting light reddened where it struck, luminous, blushing, rosy hue with purple shadows.

Then Oriane returned to her seat beside the table and looked out over the hills. Passively watched the light fade over that fat, tender countryside as she had almost every evening that she spent there, drinking sweet, heavy wine, glass after glass of it till she was dizzy and lightheaded and for the moment free of despair, completely emptied in soul, purified, roofless, open to the sun, chilled, exhilarated, hopeful even, faded, olive-green hope and the courage of the vine, but hope remained, hope, the last of the demons to leave Pandora's box.

After the sun had set, the light stayed only briefly in the sky. She looked at the orange-yellow, more yellow than orange now, on the horizon, vaguely disappointed, the blue above that had been brilliant all day faded and darkened. The ploughed earth in the vineyards and the gray leaves of the olives seemed to retain the light the longest, but darkness brewed in the shades of cypress and pine ascended from the valleys and diffused into the tranquil air.

Stupid, vain, recurring hope, what is there to hope for, forty-nine, alone with a dream that is fading, that even she had known would fade though she nourished it with every fiber of her being. All the elaborate pretending and make-believe had finally collapsed of its own weight. She was alone and had been alone from the beginning and her exhausted imagination could no longer even supply her with that shadow-man. That phantom, air-drawn, invented lover had vanished without trace or vestige save the wonder that she who had given herself in a loveless marriage for some twenty-five years with equanimity was driven to distraction in less than half a year of solitude.

She gave 500- and 1,000-lire bills to the beggars on the steps of the cathedral, to the legless man, to the dwarf-woman with the ailing baby in her arms. "You think I am a rich American but I'm poorer than you, I'd trade places with any of you." She spoke in English and under her breath, they nodded their heads without attempting to understand her and hardly a murmur of thanks. Her hand covered her mouth and she despised herself for the lies she told.

One of many lies and fantasies, as when she pressed into the church after the sweet-faced, pure-faced little nuns and knelt beside them looking for the rings on their fingers, little brides of Christ. . . . I am like them, wedded to a dream.

The birds were beginning to flit around. Birds! They were probably bats. They were undoubtedly bats, but it was too dark to really see and they moved so quickly. Little birds in the twilight, charming, but bats, winged mice really, their wings, leather-webbed elongated fingers, vicious, blind creatures with supersonic hearing.

Which was to be the subject of another one of her completely unprofitable conversations with the fat, lazy *domestica* named Rosalia who took care of her. Rosalia loathed her and she loathed Rosalia back, but communication was so laborious between them that their hostility could never come to the surface.

Bird—*uccello,* according to the dictionary, *uccellino,* little bird. Now she called the maid and pointed to the birds (bats) and said, *"Uccello? Uccellino?"* Rosalia merely looked back soberly and uncomprehendingly. *"Prego, signora?"*

"È uccello?"

She felt slightly sick to her stomach and in her distress at not being able to make herself understood she was waving her hands wildly, flapping her arms insanely. *"È uccello?"* She began to laugh hysterically. Rosalia undoubtedly thought she was pretending to be a bird herself. She folded her hands in her lap.

"Sì, uccello," said Rosalia finally. *"Gallina. Domani sera, signora."* Chicken for supper tomorrow night. Oriane shrugged helplessly and motioned impatiently to the maid to go.

She continued, nevertheless, watching the bats (birds) and fell to thinking about the young Italian who had asked her the way and then marched off in the opposite direction from the one she had indicated.

He had appeared quite suddenly on the sloping, cobbled street below the terrace and possibly he had been looking up at her for some time before he spoke. Well, she was used to it, the Italians stared and stared and they whispered behind her back, indeed they spoke boldly and openly in front of her because they knew she couldn't understand what they were saying—children do that to their poor deaf elders —*pazza, pazza, pazza,* buzz, buzz, buzz.

She could understand that much, *pazza,* crazy, *americana,* American. She was a crazy American because she lived quietly among them, took sun baths, and gave money to their beggars. Ah but she wasn't crazy. Everybody's crazy. She could see it in their eyes when they looked at her and she'd say back to them under her breath, *pazza, pazza, pazza.*

Crazy sitting in the twilight, heavy with the wine, the bottle was almost empty. She put her elbows on the table and rested her chin in her hands. Presently she would ask for some coffee and then when she had drunk almost a half liter of strong black coffee she would go indoors and the scandalized Rosalia would serve her supper. Serve her a fricasseed hen. No, tomorrow. The idiot. Ah, but she was not really crazy.

She watched the waning light, the entire valley now was dark and on the upper slopes there remained only in faint outline the ridged terraces and trailing, massed vines. The orange had almost blanched out of the sky and the yellow was diffuse and jaundiced. The rows of cypresses on a farther hill were like teeth spitting the venom of darkness into the night.

But Oriane had no use for anger either. She pressed her lips against her hand waiting for it to pass, though once she had coaxed and cultivated and nourished this anger because as far as she was concerned there was absolutely nothing else that connected her in any way with the universe. Then she had wanted to get so angry that she would run howling through the streets of the town. That would have given those Italians something to buzz about, *pazza, pazza, pazza* about. But that had been long ago, she was too tired now for anger.

Suddenly she smiled, thinking of the young Italian who had asked *her* the way. To the Via Roma, which was *a sinistra,* so he had gone off to the right.

He had come so quickly up the street. Rather, it seemed to her that he hadn't come up the street at all. She had been standing at the edge of the terrace and she would have seen him. Undoubtedly. The street approached at an angle between high walls and from where she stood (this was certainly in the strategic minds of the men who had built this fortified town) the view of every approach was completely unobstructed. Nevertheless, the young man had appeared from somewhere and had stood quietly below her looking up and then, finally, when her eyes met his, he had spoken.

His voice was soft, pitched like a conspirator's, which because she couldn't understand him she had noticed immediately. It went with his sudden, inexplicable appearance on the street, the purposeful unobtrusiveness of the huntsman—the brilliant tiger is invisible in the jungle sedges, but his posture as he stood was indolent and casual, half turned away from her, one knee thrust slightly forward, his hands at rest at his sides, only raised to gesture after he'd had to repeat his question.

Then he had gone slowly past her from left to right and she had turned her head watching him, feeling at that moment only surprise that he went so directly opposite from the way she had indicated, then noticing the halting gait, not so much in him as in his shadow that fell toward her through the red sunlight and moved with an odd stiffness over the square-cut cobbles. Which foot it was he favored it was impossible to tell, the hurt was so philosophically taken in the stride, or whether the pain was in the foot at all, or knee or hip. Now she thought she remembered also that his hand was rather stiffly held against his side, the elbow back—the jacket that he wore was ragged and a wretched fit, much too short in the sleeves, so that the hand that pressed against his rib, his wrist and half his forearm showed palely against the threadbare black cloth.

She drew the wineglass toward her on the table but she did not drink from it, instead she looked into the gleaming yellow liquid, idly noticing how it magnified and colored the cloth below, and then she smiled, thought about that hand which was so enormous, completely ill proportioned, crudely defined, a man's hand attached to a boy's slim body, but the effect was not displeasing, far from it, and the hand itself was beautiful, the glimpse she caught of it, long and narrow, strong, the fingers slightly flexed.

Rosalia came bringing the coffee. Without a word she placed the tray on the table, methodically cleared the space in front of Oriane, removed the wine bottle and the glass, emptied the ash tray, arranged the cup and saucer, the pot of coffee, the bowl of sugar, paused for a moment to see that everything was right and then just as quietly withdrew to the end of the terrace.

The maid, of course, hadn't waited to be summoned. Oriane frowned, Rosalia might have waited till she was called, but it was late, it was past the usual time, the small encounter with the Italian boy had taken a little time, and the dawdling, vague thoughts and musings had added to the hour, five minutes, ten minutes.

Rosalia had not waited to hear the chinking of a spoon against the glass, no more does a cow look at the sunset to return to the stall, nor a grape measure its shadow to swell and ripen. Not the clock but the absolute of diurnal succession, the orderly birth and death of event, a tranquillity in which there is no possibility of surprise, but merely day and night following upon each other, morning, noon, and afternoon owns each its occupations, time vanishes and eternity stands in its place.

Oriane glanced at the maid, a serene, dark shape at the edge of the terrace motionless against the sky, she wondered idly why the maid didn't go back to the kitchen as she poured herself a cup of the villainous black brew. She immediately lifted it to her lips, it was bitter and strong and hot.

Eternity surely is longer for the damned than for the blessed, she willfully tortured her lips with the scalding coffee. Her thoughts scudded dryly down the barren, rutted road of her despair, rocks and dust and fretted channels like the miserable steep mountain roads of the country, the particulars of her griefs lost in the endlessly enlarging metaphor concocted in her weary brain. She wished she were alone, she wished Rosalia would go, but was suddenly too helpless even to give that order. The coffee cooled in the cup and her sore lips turned ruefully downward at the corners. A moment later she smiled.

Irrelevantly she had thought once more of the young Italian who had inquired the way of her, *her,* a crazy man who limped, *pazzo italiano,* with the great hand pressed against his side, walking through the red sunlight, from left to right, below her on the street, his shadow fell against the rosy bricks of the cathedral wall, a purple shadow browned by the natural earth color of the flattened bricks; she wondered idly if she would see him again, fretfully, surely at the same hour on another day, for all things have their appointed time—in spite of herself she was helpless in the patterned mold, the few, dry salvages of her eccentricity were powerless to save her—he could be expected to come again, she would await his coming, the next evening and the evening after.

"Signora! Signora!"

What was it? Rosalia addressed her. Recalled her; she suddenly heard people hurrying by in the street and Rosalia calling out to her. *"Signora!"*

What? *"Cosa?"*

"Permesso?" The woman came to the table and stood awkwardly with her arms crossed over her chest. Perhaps she was cold, at night it turns cold in Italy, almost as soon as the sun is down the primordial chill rises from the earth. The maid's puffy features gleamed dimly, whitened in the dusky light from the sky, her eyes dull and black as two olives, a spasm passed over her face. *"Venga in casa, signora, prego . . . venga, venga!"*

The whole town was in the street, running and shouting, trampling and scampering, the stones rang and the walls echoed, meaningless as the migration of lemmings, *pazzi, pazzi, pazzi.* They were all crazy and the maid, Rosalia, most of all. *"Venga, venga,"* she was crying.

"Don't be ridiculous," Oriane said firmly.

Below a woman screamed and another shrieked out, "Mario, Mario!" A dog yelped sharply and somewhere in the distance bells were ringing.

"Venga in casa, venga in casa, signora!"

Oriane sat paralyzed and bewildered. *"Che cosa?"*

"Venga, signora, venga . . . signora . . . bandito . . . c'è un bandito, capisce . . . io . . ." (something) *". . . bandito. È qui nella strada . . ."* (a great rush of words, Oriane didn't catch any of them).

"No, no, non capisco!"

With "I don't understand" shutting the door against this intruding maid with her *banditi*.

Like an echo in the street, *"Banditi, banditi,"* roaring sound. "Mario, Mario!" from the screaming woman. *"Aspetti, aspetti,"* a quavering old man's voice, faltering footsteps and the sharp hitting of a cane against the pavings.

". . . briganti, signora . . . pericoloso qui . . . venga in casa, signora . . . prego . . ."

"Briganti, briganti . . . tolga Iddio . . . Mario, Mario," screaming in the street.

Oriane stood up uncertainly. She felt dizzy and heavy, the shouting seemed to come from a long way off, even the fat maid standing before her gesticulating wildly and giving out floods of words seemed distant and unsubstantial.

She waited. Presently the street quieted, everyone had gone by and left the street, there was no one left to come, there was no one to shout and run. Echo from farther down, distant, "Mario, Mario!"

"Briganti, signora, banditi, è pericoloso. Venga in casa," Rosalia repeated loudly.

175

Oriane smiled. At last she understood, the maid wanted her to go into the house, it was dangerous, perilous on the terrace because of the bandits and brigands. The maid seeing the comprehension on her face exploded into torrents of words and exclamations and hurriedly began to pile the coffee things back on the tray.

"No," Oriane exclaimed.

"Prego?"

"Io desidero stare qui." She seized the tray with both hands and held it fast.

"Signora!" the maid wailed imploringly.

Oriane raised her voice. "It's okay. I want to stay here. I'm not afraid of the bandits."

Suddenly she clapped her hands to her mouth. *"Dov'è dov'è?"*

"Nella strada."

"Adesso? Now, now, he's in the street?"

The maid spoke laboriously, pausing between each word. *"Lei lo ha veduto, signora."* She pointed at Oriane. *"Lei ha parlato con lui . . ."* (a whole sentence she couldn't understand).

She understood enough. Now she seized the maid by the shoulder, desperately half pulling, half pushing, forced her to the edge of the terrace, pointed down below to the spot where the young Italian had stood staring up, a handsome, gentle face, softened by the rosy light. *"Là? Là?"*

"Sì, signora, colà. Lo stesso."

"È andato a sinistra." She was no longer confused, *a destra,* to the right, *sinistra,* left, sinister. *"A sinistra."* Desperate lie in a tongue she could not speak. She pointed to the left.

176

"No, signora, è andato a destra. Guarda!"

She leaned out looking where the maid indicated
past the jutting wall of the cathedral (remembered
mottling on the wall where the stucco gone revealed
bare, earth-colored bricks, a black wall now against the
dimly lighted, sloping street).

Down to the crowded square at the bottom, she could
only see the smallest part of it, filled with the black mass
of people, a corner of the square and a section of the
floodlit orange façade of the Signorial Palace.

Suddenly she broke away from the maid and was
running down the steps from the terrace.

"Signora! Signora!"

She stumbled on the street but caught herself against
a grating and hurried clumsily, blindly over the slip-
pery, squared cobbles, toward the distant beaming light,
to the shouting and the people.

"Così Iddio vi aiuti, signora!"

Coatless, hatless, in awkward high-heeled shoes, her
hair streaming out behind her, hurrying, crying out
herself, she rushed headlong. For what? Impelled,
drawn forward helplessly by the crowd ahead, caught by
the same force that had swept those others into the
square, uncomprehending, her wits dazzled and dazed,
eagerly hastening, gasping for breath, her lungs burning, the gulped air rattling in her throat. Her footing on
the street was precarious, not only the uneven paving,
but the double slope, down to the square and sideways
toward a central gutter, the tall buildings rising
abruptly without sidewalks seemed to press down on
her.

"Signora, signora," Rosalia still called, for she was
still in the sight of her own terrace. The young Italian

had come secretly, by stealth up the open passageway, inexplicably invisible in motion, to stand suddenly below, remaining but the few seconds that it took to ask the way, then moving slowly away, his shadow halt and black in the red sunlight.

The square was lighted with the brilliant glaring white of the floods placed on the roofs of the buildings opposite the Signorial Palace, blinding light, the people surged about her, she struggled blindly through them; she saw that men and boys had climbed the lampposts and to the top of the equestrian statue in the middle of the square. Directly ahead of her on the steps of the palace was a small squadron of police, like guardsmen on a stage, brilliantly accoutered. (She had laughed at them when she had first seen them marching by as if on parade, they were chiefly impressive because there were so few of them, flamboyantly military as becomes the representatives of law and order in the lawless hills and prudently ineffective; they had strutted up the street, not quite in step, accompanied by skipping troops of little boys.) Now they stood grimly facing the crowd with fixed bayonets held in front of them.

She had thrown herself heedlessly into the crowd, floundered helplessly in it, pressed in on all sides by these dark, alien beings who even now in the excitement drew back a little from this thrusting, gaunt creature who had placed herself in their midst; thus she inched forward slowly through the mass of people where here and there they gave way in amazement and left a little space.

Then at last she stood at the edge of the fountain; water spouted from the mouths of leaping dolphins, and from hidden outlets over reclining sea nymphs and river gods, into a wide, round basin, green and veined with ripples. On the far side, black against the paleness of the marble and the water, lay the figure of a man, his head and shoulders were slightly raised, supported by the foot-high parapet that enclosed the fountain; one great hand hung down, plunged into the water. His head was thrown back and his eyes softly closed as if in sleep; spray shone in his dark hair, and a small trickling of blood, bright, innocent redness in a narrow line from his temple.

Only for a second she looked and saw. He was the hunted then, not the brilliant hunter.

The pain of lameness was ignored in the desperation of extremity, not spirit, the hand and the arm extending from the ragged coat clapped to the heart a mortal wound. He had required of her the way.

"*A sinistra, signora.*"

Yes, of course, sinister, ill omened.

The faces beyond this fallen one were not the faces of men; of fierce wolves and foxes, of greedy swine that falls upon its farrow, brutish, ululant cries came from their throats. Exultant that a man's death came in a boy's slim years.

"*Venga, signora, venga.*" She was teetering at the edge of the fountain, someone had seized her from in back and held her steady. "This is no place for Signora," the voice shouted in her ear. "Come, Missus."

"Yes." She submitted and suffered without question to the hands that supported her and pulled her away. A broad man made the path for her through the crowd and drew her through it.

"It is a pity for Missus should see." Dazedly she recognized him as one of the clerks at the hotel, she only knew that he spoke English, that his eyes were very small and surprisingly blue, struck her as kind and also dishonest.

"Don't be afraid, Missus, the bandit can do no more bad things." They reached the edge of the square and the empty entrance to her street, now he let go of her arm to gesture. "He is finished with doing bad. The people don't have to be frightened now."

He had a very wide, flat nose and under it a little black mustache, suddenly the nose and mustache twitched. Like a rabbit. Who's afraid?

"I can go on from here, thank you very much."

"I will go with you but there is nothing to be afraid of, Missus."

"No, no, I'll be all right."

"Very good, Missus, *buona sera*." He bowed stiffly from the hips.

"*Buona sera*."

She saw him go back into the crowd, he was eager to go. He will pick the dead boy's pockets. Never mind, yet he is a good man. She turned and started wearily up the hill.

When she was opposite the cathedral, the bells began to ring. She shrank into a doorway and put her hands to her ears. The young Italian had gone past her to the right and around the side wall of this same building. He might have stood where she was standing now.

The bells, tremendous jangling ringing, strident brass and bronze and piercing silver bells, sounding from the campanile not fifteen feet from where she stood, barbarous clanging, unbearable racketing summons made to resound over the miles of shadowed hills and valleys, to the farthest hut and farmhouse, to sound the hour according to the canon, over the babyish blatting of goats and sheep that the shepherd drives on the road, the yells of children in the courtyards, the squealing of pigs and clacking of chickens, bellows of asses and cows and oxen.

And the solemn, pealing reverberation should still be heard in the noisy square where the people shouted and the dead man lay, loudly ring bells to drown out the crying voices celebrating the death of the outcast.

Oriane was deafened and appalled by the fearful sound struck off the rigid bells virtually in her ear, so close by that the energy of the concussion vibrated in the pavement under her feet, in the wall she leaned against, clanging, thunderous bells awakening echoes in her head so that the uproar of sound became a boiling turmoil within and without, pressing against her ear-drums, the fantastic cacophony inside the bony passages of her head hopelessly seeking egress to be crowded back by fresh tintinnabulations, metal on metal crushing the tender nerve without let or mercy. Uselessly she covered her ears with her hands and stopped them up, she drowned in the hell of unquiet, she suffocated in the inferno of sound.

Suddenly she ran across the street into the cathedral. It was dark here and the bells were somewhat muffled, she stood just inside the red curtain staring at the white figure of Christ on the Cross.

A thin, emaciated, great-boned Christ, larger than life, rendered by an artist who had spared no pains to represent each anguish and torture, slack cheeks and sagging body twisting away from the spike-riven feet, tied at the elbows, nailed at the palms, great brown thorns thrust down on the bloody forehead, the spear wound, gaping and open, glistening eyeballs were turned upwards, the mouth open and screaming. Oriane looked away.

To the right was a small shrine brightly lighted with candles to the Holy Virgin. Oriane thrust her hands into the pockets of her dress looking for a coin. He was probably a Catholic, I'll light a candle for him.

An old woman in black and heavily shawled brushed by her, and then a second woman. They went to the font and crossed themselves, they paused briefly in the aisle and genuflected.

Her pockets were quite empty. Suddenly her eyes filled with tears and she sank to her knees in the corner by the curtain. The bell ringer had finished his task and the tower was silent, but she could still hear the ringing. Her eyes were closed and her hands covered her face, but she could still see the candles and the figure on the Cross.

He wouldn't come again. She had thought he would come again, she would have waited for him to come.

He is dead. He could have saved me but he died.

She scrambled to her feet and ran from the cathedral. He died. He could have saved me. He is dead.